Just One Time

Samantha Baca

Just One Time

Second Chances

Third Time's The Charm

Four-ever Single

Fifth Wheel

Cover Design: Richard Baca
Image(s): DepositPhotos

Contents

Contents

One
Abby

"Here's your tall cinnamon dolce latte with no foam and grande black tea." I handed the to-go cups to the beautifully pregnant woman, who took them and smiled at her magazine-perfect looking husband with a dazzling smile. Once they were gone, I let out the breath I had been holding and muttered *lucky bitch,* under my breath.

I had totally forgotten that Nate was still there, perched on the end of the counter, drinking his black coffee out of a ceramic mug because he insisted that it tasted better. Since he had nowhere to rush off to, he didn't need a to-go cup.

"Why's she so lucky?" he asked, pulling me out of my jealous-induced daydream and back into the present.

I shrugged and wiped the counter down, knowing that it was already clean but needing the distraction from his question.

"Come on, Abby, what's up?" He hopped down from the counter and set his empty coffee cup on the tray for the busser to grab on his way back.

"Nothing," I lied.

He raised a brow and shoved his hands into his pockets, rocking back on his heels as he waited for me to come clean.

I arched mine back at him, watching the dimples in his

cheeks as his grin spread across his stupidly gorgeous face. It wasn't just the emerald green eyes that drew me in or the short dark hair that looked soft enough to run my hands through—which I had plenty of times over the years—but it was the light in his eyes and the way that he watched me that made a swarm of butterflies shoot through my stomach.

Nate Wilson had been my best friend since we were seven years old and some mean boy on the playground stole my fruit snacks and pulled my skirt up for everyone to see my days of the week underwear. Nate had bravely stepped in and defended me, and we had been inseparable ever since.

My mom always thought it was cute that we were so close and hoped that someday we would fall in love and get married. On the other hand, my dad couldn't understand why I didn't want to be friends with any of the girls in Beaumont Creek and prayed that I wouldn't end up knocked up like one of those girls on TV. I had rolled my eyes at the thought back then, but now that my biological clock was ticking loud enough for the small town of Beaumont Creek to hear, I kinda wished that maybe I had been that lucky back then after all.

"Earth to Abby," he teased, leaning his forearms on the counter to look up at me.

I tucked a strand of hair behind my ear and felt the blush creeping up my neck at the thought of having a baby with Nate. I suddenly wished I hadn't cut my hair in a rash decision last week when I approached my fortieth birthday. If it were the same long, blonde locks that I had kept since high school, I would be able to sweep them over my shoulder and hide my embarrassment.

"I swear, it's nothing. It's stupid, and I didn't think you could hear me," I laughed before taking my towel and playfully hitting his arm with it. "I forgot that you were still sitting there."

"I'm always here, and I hear everything." His grin spread even further across his face.

"What does she have that you don't?"

"I don't know," I snorted. "Everything? A gorgeous husband who obviously adores her. A baby on the way. A body that will probably bounce back to model status the second she shoots that thing out of her overly perfect vagina that won't endure any damage during delivery and will have her husband begging for another baby the second he sees it." I let the last few words fall out as I finished the longest run-on sentence I had ever heard.

"You got all of that from the few minutes they were in here to order coffee?" he asked, not focusing on any of the ridiculous things I had just said.

I shrugged again, knowing that it was stupid and ridiculous.

"Just because she has those things doesn't mean that she's lucky."

"I know," I said quietly, looking up at the *Rockin' Rooster* sign above the door. It was old and barely hanging on the rickety nail that my grandpa had put it up with many years ago. I knew that eventually, I would need to replace it and update everything else in the café, but I just couldn't bring myself to do it.

"Is this because you just turned forty?" he asked gently.

I hung my head and shook it even though we both knew it was a lie.

"There's nothing wrong with getting older," he lied.

"Really?" I countered with another raised brow. "Because I'm pretty sure that my eggs are all shriveling up and dying inside, along with my chances of finding someone I love and want to settle down and start a family with. It's not like Beaumont Creek has many eligible bachelors my age coming to town and looking to sweep the local barista off of her tired, swollen feet."

"It will happen, Abby."

"How do you know?"

"I don't," he shrugged. "But I have faith that everything will work out the way it's supposed to."

I walked out from behind the counter and over to one of the tables that looked out the window to Main Street as Nate joined me.

"Do you know what my mother said after I blew out the candles on my cake?" I asked, looking at him.

"What?"

"She said, be careful, dear; you wouldn't want to exert yourself trying to blow all of those candles out. Then she paused and laughed when she said, *better yet, maybe that would help land a man.*"

His brow furrowed as he processed it.

"She thinks I should advertise that I'm good at blowing things," I blurted out.

His face turned a sudden shade of red before he composed himself and tried to hide his laugh behind his fist.

"Well, are you?" he asked.

"Nate!" I gasped, looking around to make sure no one could hear him.

"I mean if we're going to start advertising that, we should at least make sure it's true."

"I am not answering that, and shame on you for asking." I shook my head and pointed a finger at him.

"Can't blame me for trying," he laughed. "I was just trying to be a good best friend and get on board with project *Abby Blows*."

"We are not calling it that, and there's no project. There is no one in this teeny tiny town that I would even consider dating, let alone have a kid with."

"We can always try other towns and see how they feel about *Abby Blows*."

"No," I laughed. "And you'd better stop calling it that."

"I don't think we should get into any more detail," he joked. "People might be taken aback by that. You want to start slowly and ease them in."

"Are we still talking about the same thing?" I laughed. "Because now it's starting to sound a bit like directions."

Another blush flashed across his face, and I felt satisfied that I was able to get to him. Witty banter was our thing, but he was usually the one who could get me to shut up by embarrassing me first, so I was truly enjoying this newfound victory.

"The right guy is out there, Abby. You just have to be patient."

"Easy for you to say," I sighed. "You have women practically throwing their panties at the *hottest firefighter* in Beaumont Creek. You don't have any problem getting dates, let alone finding a woman who wants you to put a baby in them."

"Hottest *Captain*," he corrected with a wink. "And there's no one I would be willing to date or put a baby in. They're all either as old as my mother or young enough to need a fake ID to get into a liquor store."

"Well, at least you're still hot."

"That's mostly because I'm running in and out of fires. You'd be hot too. The gear combined with the flames—you get the picture."

"Funny," I joked childishly. "You still have women who want you."

"And you have men who want you."

"And yet neither of us want the ones who want us," I replied cheekily.

Something flashed across Nate's face, but it was gone before I could tell what it was.

"So, what are your other options?" he asked, changing the subject.

"What do you mean?"

"For your *dried-up* eggs. Can you freeze them until you're ready?"

"I can, but that costs money, and I don't know that I want to wait that long to have a baby. What if I don't meet anyone until I'm fifty or sixty?"

"You're going to meet someone before then."

"Who knows."

"Can't you do that insemination thing?"

"IVF? Yeah," I exhaled heavily. "I talked to my doctor about it a few weeks ago, and she gave me the name of a specialist that I can go to if I want to look into it, but I'm not going to."

"Why not?"

I leaned back against the chair and watched the children playing on the playground at the elementary school across the street. My heart ached at the thought of never having my own children; each year that passed was a constant reminder of what I dreamed of but couldn't have.

"It's super expensive for one," I said sadly. "Even if I could pull the money together, I don't think I would want to have a baby with a stranger that I would never know. How would I answer their questions growing up about who their dad was? I feel like I need to know who the person is and that I would want them to be involved in our lives, to watch their child grow up with me."

He reached across the table and squeezed my hand.

"I'm sorry, Abby."

"Don't be; it's not your fault I haven't found *the one* yet." I wiped a tear away with the back of my hand as the door opened and the rooster above it let out a weak-sounding crowing. I smiled and waved at the customers, letting them have a few minutes to look over the menu before deciding.

While Beaumont Creek was a super small town, we were close to Cape May, which brought several tourists through as they eventually made their way to Ocean City, New Jersey.

"I better get up there," I said, pulling my hand away before standing up and pushing the chair back under the table.

"Alright, well, I'm heading to town to run some errands. Do you need anything?"

"Nothing that you can buy," I laughed.

"Try to cheer up, Abby. It'll all work out. You'll see."

He gave me his award-winning smile and then headed out the door.

Two
Nate

It broke my heart to see the sadness in Abby's eyes this morning as she confided in me. It wasn't a secret that she wanted to get married and have a family, but I hadn't known it was bothering her that much now that she had turned forty.

My birthday was a few weeks before hers, and while I had noticed that she seemed a little down about it, she hadn't said anything until now. If I could give her what she wanted, I would in a heartbeat. Anything to make her happy.

I ran my errands in town, rolled the windows down, and enjoyed the fresh air on my way back to Beaumont Creek. I had sent Abby a text message earlier, asking about her dinner plans, and she responded with an emoji of a bowl of pasta which meant that she was making macaroni and cheese out of a box. I made another quick stop at the farmer's market, then headed to her house.

It was after six, and her car was in the driveway when I got there. I had already dropped my stuff off at home but brought the groceries I had picked up and two bottles of Abby's favorite wine.

I knocked on the door and then pushed it open, knowing that she was already expecting me and would have unlocked the door a few minutes ago. She was singing in the kitchen as she reached on her tiptoes to pull a box of macaroni down from the top shelf. Her shorts rode up dangerously high to show just the hint of her perky, round ass, and her shirt lifted enough that I saw the tanned skin that kissed her curvy body.

"Need help?" I offered as more of a way to let her know that I was there, not that I was going to let her make the boxed pasta.

She turned around and pointed a spatula at me.

"You're just the person I need," she said happily, handing me the spatula as she moved to the side to let me into her space.

I smiled and lifted slightly, grabbing the box with ease without the need for the spatula. I set it on the counter and then planted a kiss on her head.

"You're so frustratingly good at that," she muttered, grabbing the box.

"Good at what?" I asked, a grin tugging at the corners of my mouth.

"Everything." She set the box down and looked up at me.

"Well, I'm just taller than you. That's all."

"You make it look so easy with your muscles and lean body that doesn't strain to do anything."

I paused for a moment before I said anything.

Was she checking me out and commenting on my body?

"I just know how to get the job done," I winked.

Her cheeks flushed, and her eyes darted away from me as

she picked up on the innuendo I hadn't meant to put down.

"You hungry?" she asked, holding the box of macaroni and cheese in the air and shaking it at me.

"We're not eating that."

"We're not?" She looked from me to the box, then back to me. "Why not?"

"Because I don't eat that stuff unless I have to. And usually, that's only when we have a new rookie who doesn't know how to cook."

"Well, I don't have anything else. I haven't been to the store yet, so it's either this or a possibly expired can of soup that I found a few minutes ago while trying to get this bad boy down."

"Not to worry, I brought reinforcements." I walked back over to the door and picked up the two paper bags filled with groceries that I had brought in with me.

"What's that?" she asked, leaning up on her tiptoes to see what was inside.

"It's a surprise," I laughed, pulling the bags away so she couldn't see.

She frowned and pouted, reminding me of when I first met her as this sassy seven-year-old who ruled the world around her.

I set the bags down on the counter and pulled out the two bottles of wine.

"Here," I said, handing one to her. "Why don't you work on opening the wine, and I'll take care of dinner."

She smiled and took them.

"Thank you; you didn't have to do all of this. I was more than fine with macaroni."

"I know, that's what scares me," I teased and bent down to grab a pan.

"Hey, I have standards," she laughed. "Just not when it comes to dinner for myself."

"You make fantastic food all day for everyone else; it's okay to let someone cook for you. Besides, we still need to celebrate your birthday, and you keep avoiding it."

"That's because it doesn't need to be celebrated," she sighed, cutting the foil on the wine before opening it, the pop in the air a satisfying sound. "I turned a year older, that's all. Just one more step further away from my youth and the possibility of making any of my dreams come true."

"It's not that bad," I reminded her as I started pulling the groceries out of the bag and then sent her on her way to the couch with her glass of wine. I took a sip of mine and then got to work on making dinner.

Thirty minutes later, the food was ready, and her house smelled delicious from the roasted garlic and steak that I had cooked in the oven. Abby immediately dove into her baked potato before piercing a green bean with her fork and slowly pushing it into her mouth as she took bites.

I tried to look away, but there was something so sexy about how she looked as she slightly parted her lips to take in each bite. She moaned quietly as she ate, and I couldn't help but think about what she would sound like if I were the one to make her moan instead.

It was ridiculous to think about her this way, but if I was being honest with myself, I had been into Abby since we were teens, and she finally grew into the body that every man wanted to get his hands on once she was twenty-one and started hanging out in the only bar in town. But I didn't need alcohol to know that she was attractive—I saw it every single day and was relieved when her party days ended as quickly as they had started so I wasn't tempted to punch anyone in the face for ogling her in front of me.

"This is so good. Thank you, Nate," she said, finishing her bite before taking a sip of wine.

Her glass was almost empty, so I got up, grabbed the bottle from the island, and refilled it.

"How was the rest of your day?" I asked, hoping to get her talking so I didn't have to watch her eat anything else until I could get my stupid dick under control.

"It was fine. Lunch was busier than usual, which helped keep my mind off everything."

I had wanted to steer the conversation further away from this but knew that she wouldn't be bringing it up if she didn't want to keep talking about it.

I took a bite of steak and chewed, giving her the space to guide the conversation to wherever she wanted it to go.

"I talked to my sister today, and she had a wild idea," she said nervously, taking another drink of wine.

Her face flushed red as her honey brown eyes widened with something that looked almost like fear mixed with excitement.

"Oh yeah?" I replied slowly, trying to get a feel for where this was going. "What was it?"

She lifted her glass and tilted her head back to finish the rest of her wine. When she was done, she set the glass down on the table and kept her fingers wrapped tightly around the stem before letting go and looking at me.

"She, umm, she thought that maybe I didn't need to do IVF to have a baby."

"Okay…"

"She said that there might be another way to do it. You know, one that wouldn't cost as much, and I would know who the father was."

I felt my spine tingle and knew where she was going with this.

"I just need someone who's willing to give me a *sample* of their best swimmers. No strings attached. It wouldn't have to be awkward or anything."

"Just a sample?" I raised a brow and leaned back against the chair, pushing my plate away.

I folded my arms and watched her squirm nervously.

"Just one time—that's all."

"So you want to do like a turkey-baster type thing? Is she going to inject it into you?"

She was mid-sip when she spit her wine across the table.

"Oh my God, I'm so sorry!" She jumped and grabbed a towel to clean up the mess on the table.

I laughed, finally feeling a little relaxed, and helped her.

"Sorry, I was just trying to visualize what you were saying."

Her eyes widened, and I realized what I had said.

"Okay—take that back. I wasn't trying to get a visual of you—just the process you were talking about with your *sample of best swimmers.*"

"It's a stupid idea," she groaned, sitting down and tossing the towel on the table between us. "I don't even know anyone I could ask, so it doesn't matter anyway."

I took a drink of my wine and counted to ten. That's what you were supposed to do before you rushed into something stupid, right?

She lowered her head, and the light caught her eyes. The brilliance that usually radiated from them was no longer there. There was no spark that lit up her face, and I could see the sadness that had overcome her.

I took another drink and then exhaled heavily, hoping that I would blow out any apprehensions along with it.

"I'll do it," I said, startling her with how loud my voice suddenly was.

She tilted her head to the side and studied me as if I had lost my mind. *I probably did.*

"What?" she whispered.

"I'll do it. I'll give you some of my best swimmers."

16

Three
Abby

"You're kidding me, right?" I snorted, trying not to choke on my wine.

"No, I'm dead serious."

"Nate—this isn't like loaning me twenty dollars or filling up my car because I ran out of gas again."

"I know."

"It's a baby. Like a real *baby*."

He nodded his head and leaned back in his chair. I could feel his foot tapping anxiously on the tile and wondered if he was getting ready to bolt and retract his offer.

"I wasn't meaning you," I stammered, lying through my teeth. "Jane and I didn't get into details about *who* it should be, just that there were *other* options out there."

He didn't say anything, but the look on his face said he knew that I was lying. The truth was that Jane and I had gone into *very* specific detail about how wonderful it would be to have Nate be the one who I had a baby with. I loved him. I trusted him. He was good-looking, and his family didn't have any serious medical problems that I knew of. Heck, his grandparents were thriving and living their best lives in their nineties, so good genes seemed to run in his family. Not to mention that our baby would be freaking a-dor-a-ble.

After a few minutes of awkward silence, I sighed and said, "I'm sorry. I shouldn't have passive-aggressively hinted about it and then turned around and lied about it."

"I know you too well for you to lie to me," he teased with a single shoulder shrug.

I rolled my eyes. This was true, so there was no point in denying it.

"I'm still embarrassed that I even brought it up, to begin with."

"Why?"

I raised my brows and stared at him as if he had eight heads.

"Why? Because it's not every day that you ask your best friend for some of their sperm so you can have a baby," I said with a ghost of a smile. It wasn't that I found the situation funny, but he was grinning like the cat who ate the canary, and his smile was infectious.

"You've asked me for worse," he teased.

"I have not!" I laughed.

"Have too."

"Like what?"

"Remember that time you convinced me to drive you to the gas station at almost midnight so you could get sushi?"

I groaned and closed my eyes. That was by far the *worst* idea I'd ever had, and the food poisoning proved it. I still cringed when I thought about gas station sushi.

"Or how about when you asked me to drive you to Cape May so you could meet up with that asshole who kept standing you up?"

"He was an asshole," I agreed. "And he made me pay for dinner because he 'forgot his wallet'."

"Or how about the time that you *desperately* wanted something but didn't trust me enough to come out and ask me to help you?"

The playful tone he had a few minutes ago was gone. His eyes softened around the edges as he watched me.

"I do trust you, but this is a lot to ask of you—of anyone—unless I go to a sperm bank and just pick a vial."

"But that's not what you want, and you know it."

"I know," I sighed.

"I'm telling you that I'll do this with you, Abby. I'll help you make a baby."

I pushed the breath out that I had been holding and allowed my lungs to deflate for a few seconds before I sucked in another breath.

"I don't know how this would even work," I blurted out. "I'm sure it'll get expensive with all of the appointments."

"What are you talking about?" he asked, his brows pulled together.

"Well, we'll have to get a sample from you, and then I think they have to retrieve some of my eggs. Or maybe they can just inject it inside of me? I don't know; there's a lot that we would have to look into."

He rubbed his lips together as he tried to keep from laughing.

"What's so funny?" I laughed, feeling a little defensive. "There's a lot that has to happen for this to work. You would have the easy job."

"Or…."

"Or what?"

"We could just do it the old-fashioned way."

I pulled my head back in surprise. There was no way he was proposing *that,* was he?

"Like…"

He nodded and chewed his bottom lip.

"I'm going to need you to say it." My voice was as shaky as my knees.

He released his lip and leaned forward, resting his forearms on the table.

"We have sex, and I get you pregnant without any medical intervention."

Heat washed over me in waves, making me feel dizzy from what he was proposing.

"Sex?" I asked when I was finally able to speak again.

"Yes. That is how most babies are conceived."

"With you?"

"Unless you wanted me to find you someone else? I gotta admit—that might go into the stack of terrible things you've asked me for." He arched a brow playfully.

"We can't have sex," I laughed.

"Why not?"

"Because what if it's weird?"

"Why would it be weird? Do you have some strange, kinky fetishes that I don't know about? Because believe it or not—I might be into it." He wiggled his eyebrows.

Hearing him say *kinky* and *fetishes* sent a tingle up my spine and created a warmth between my legs that I hadn't expected.

"I don't want to ruin our friendship…."

"I don't want that either," he agreed. "We can try it and see if it works. Just one time, if it doesn't work—or it gets awkward—then we can move to plan B. But at least with my way, you won't have to spend any money, and you get a guaranteed orgasm."

"Just one time?" I confirmed nervously, trying not to focus too much on the orgasm part. *When was the last time I had one of those?*

"We'll never know unless we try."

I tapped my fingers on the table while I considered it. There were a lot of terrible decisions that I had made in my life but sleeping with Nate didn't feel like one. If anything, I felt excited by the idea of it, and that probably scared me more than anything. We were about to cross a line that we couldn't come back from if this didn't work out.

What would happen if I didn't get pregnant? Would we try again? He said *just one time,* but what if we needed another try? Would he be willing to do it with me again? Was this something he wanted or was he just doing it to help me out? Did he even want kids?? I couldn't remember ever having that conversation with him, but now didn't feel like the right time to ask him.

"So, what do you think? Do you wanna try?" he asked, breaking me from my fog.

"Just one time," I confirmed, feeling my body light up with a deadly combination of excitement and nerves.

Four
Nate

You would think that I had suggested that we go out and run over a basket of puppies with the shocked look that was still sitting on Abby's face after I proposed that we have sex together. I knew it was a crazy idea, but honestly—it made the most sense. We both agreed that this would give her everything she wanted—a baby with someone that she knew, trusted, and who would be involved in the baby's life. The only part that we were eliminating from the original plan was having a doctor stick a turkey baster up there to knock her up.

We were both on our third glasses of wine while I tried to get a feel for how she was taking everything. If she changed her mind and decided not to do this, that would be fine. No lines would be drawn; no boundaries would be crossed. This would just be one of those things that we looked back at later on and laughed about.

She was sitting on the couch with her legs curled under her while pretending to watch TV. I knew that she wasn't actually watching it because her eyes were glued to the screen, and I had never once seen Abby watch the evening news. It always depressed her so she would change the channel to a rerun of whatever sitcom she could find.

I shifted on the other end of the couch, debating whether

to ask her how she was doing or wait it out until she was ready to talk. She lifted her glass and took a sip, her eyes still fixated on the news. I got up and went to the bathroom, needing a moment to stretch my legs.

When I came back, she was in the kitchen rinsing her glass before setting it in the sink. I walked up behind her and put my hand on her shoulder, the way I always did when I knew that she was upset or stressed.

She flung around, startled by my touch. I pulled my hand away and took a step back to give her space.

"I'm sorry," she said, holding a hand to her chest. "You startled me."

"Sorry, I didn't mean to."

"It's okay, I've just been a little out of my element tonight. *Obviously,*" she muttered the last word under her breath.

I leaned back against the island behind me.

"Do you want to talk about it?"

"I honestly don't know where to start," she laughed. "There's a lot that I need to think about and consider."

I nodded and watched as a single tear rolled down her cheek.

"Come here," I said softly, pulling her into me. She wrapped her arms around my waist while I held her, gently rubbing her back. "It's all going to be okay. You don't have to decide anything tonight."

"I know," she murmured against my chest. "If this is something I want, why does it feel so scary?"

"Because this time it's real. It's not you daydreaming about it, it's you having to decide if you want to take this next step in your life. It's a huge change, Abby, and one that you shouldn't take lightly. Take time to think about it—write down the pros and cons if you need to—but my offer will still be there at the end of the day. You don't have to rush through this."

She squeezed me tighter before pulling back and smiling up at me.

"I love you," she said before leaning up to kiss my cheek.

I turned my head at the same time, and instead of kissing my cheek, her lips brushed against mine. I felt the spark at the same time she did because instead of pulling away, she paused for a second before kissing me again.

This time the kiss was deliberate as she moved her mouth against mine, whimpering when my tongue slid across her lip, begging for access.

I wrapped my hand around the back of her head, holding her in place as my tongue eagerly explored, tasting the sweet wine mixed with everything I imagined she would taste like.

Her hands rubbed my chest as I lowered mine down her back until they hovered inches above her ass. I wanted more but didn't want to make a move unless I knew she was okay with it.

Suddenly she reached behind her and pushed them down to her plump cheeks, letting me know that was exactly where she wanted them. I grabbed handfuls of ass and felt the strain of my erection against my jeans as she pressed her body tighter against mine.

I kissed her deeper, eager for more. Now that I had tasted her, I couldn't imagine not doing this with her ever again. I wanted her more than I had ever wanted anything before in my life.

She pulled away, panting as we both tried to catch our breath. I nudged her head to the side and slowly kissed her neck, letting my tongue run along her smooth skin down to her shoulder.

"Abby," I breathed as a warning.

"I want this, Nate," she panted, grabbing the bottom of my shirt before pulling it up and over my head. "I don't want to think about it—I just want to do it."

"I need you to be clearer," I moaned against her neck as I worked my way up the other side. "Tell me what you want, Abby."

"I want you to fuck me. Now."

I tucked my fingers under her ass and lifted her to my hips as she wrapped her legs around me. I had spent plenty of time in Abby's house to know the way to her bedroom without looking. She giggled as I squeezed her ass cheeks and then slowly slid her down my body onto the bed, making sure she felt my erection through my jeans on her way down.

"Are you sure?" I asked as she slid up the bed and shimmied out of her shorts.

She looked me in the eye, pulled her bottom lip in between her teeth, and then lifted her shirt over her head and tossed it across the room. Then, without looking away, she unhooked her bra in the back, teasing me as she held the cups to her chest.

I had imagined what Abby would look like naked a million times since I was a hormonal teenager, but now I was finally going to find out. She laid down and held the bra with one hand while she curled her finger into a come-hither motion and called me over.

I never took my eyes off her as I stepped out of my jeans and hooked my thumbs into my briefs before sliding them down my thighs. Her eyes were glued to every movement and widened when she saw how big I was when I tried to cover my dick with one hand.

She swallowed hard, then looked up at me.

This was really going to happen.

I crawled onto the bed beside her and laid on my side, studying her beautiful face.

"One more time, Abby—are you sure this is what you want?"

"I'm sure, Nate."

She wrapped a hand around my neck, pulling me down to her. I closed my eyes as our lips met again and allowed my hands to roam her body.

I gently nudged her hand out of the way before grabbing the fabric of her bra and tossing it to the floor. I pulled away from the kiss and looked down, taking in the pure perfection beneath me.

"You're so fucking beautiful," I whispered before running my tongue across her chest. I lazily traced circles around each nipple, smiling when it would harden against my touch before pulling it into my mouth and sucking.

"That feels amazing," she moaned, arching her back.

"You're amazing," I countered, still unable to believe I was about to have sex with Abby.

While my tongue was busy playing with her nipples, I ran my hand down her stomach and let it dip inside her panties. She was wet and ready for me, making it easy to slip a finger inside. We both gasped simultaneously, her pussy clenching tightly around my finger.

I promised her an orgasm, and I hadn't been lying. At this rate, I would spend the rest of my life giving her as many as her gorgeous body could handle because the sound of her moaning my name was the best song I had ever heard, and the way her body responded to me had forever ruined me for any other woman.

I fucked her with my finger for a few minutes before adding another one. She tensed beneath me before she quickly adjusted and scratched her nails down my back. I increased the pace, sliding in and out with more pressure while my thumb rubbed against her clit. She was close, I could feel it.

A few more swipes of my thumb, and I felt the first spasms of her pussy as it clenched against me as she screamed out my name and arched up off the bed. I kept going until she fell back against the mattress and whimpered my name once more.

I pulled my fingers out and studied her post-orgasm face. Her cheeks were flushed, and her eyes slightly hooded while her chest rose and fell heavily as she tried to catch her breath.

"I want more," she said with a smile. "Now I know what you're packing, and I want it."

She nodded to my erection which was jutting up to my stomach. I grabbed it with my fist and stroked it a few times while she watched.

"Is this what you want?"

She licked her lips and nodded.

"How do you want it?"

"However you want to give it to me. There are condoms in the top drawer."

I raised a brow and waited to see if she really wanted me to use one. While we hadn't technically planned for this to happen right now, it was an opportunity to get what she wanted.

"Oh. Duh." She closed her eyes and smacked her palm against her forehead. "Never mind that and bring your big cock over here."

"Oooh, you're a dirty talker, aren't you?" I teased as I climbed on top of her and held my dick at her entrance.

"I'll say whatever you want me to," she laughed, squirming beneath me as she eagerly tried to slide me inside of her.

"That's good to know."

I locked eyes with her as I slowly slid inside. She gasped loudly, and I stopped for a moment so she could adjust to my size. Once she started breathing again, I moved slowly so I didn't hurt her. A few minutes later, I was fully seated inside of her but had to fight the urge to fuck her the way I wanted to until she was ready.

I lowered my chest to hers and kissed the side of her neck, feeling her relax against my touch.

"Are you okay?" I whispered in her ear.

"Yeah, I'm good."

"If it hurts, you have to tell me."

"Okay."

I pumped slowly, letting her adjust to the motion before she lifted her legs and rested them against my chest, giving me more access. I closed my eyes and moaned when I felt how deep I was inside of her. I rocked into her gently, pleased when she started grinding her hips against me to get more friction.

Everything with Abby felt different, so I wasn't surprised that this would too. The problem was that I hadn't expected it to feel like *this*. It didn't feel like we were just fucking— it felt like we were making love. Everything was gentle and tender as we moved together, and I never wanted it to end. Her eyes fluttered open, and I felt something snap inside of me. It was at that moment that I realized I was already past the point of no return and that I was head-over-heels in love with my best friend.

Five
Abby

"That was amazing," I panted as I laid on my back and felt Nate roll over beside me. We were both panting and out of breath. I was about to jump up and head to the bathroom when a thought suddenly stopped me.

"What's wrong?" he asked, turning his head to look at me.

"Nothing."

"You're lying. I can tell. What's wrong?"

I tilted my head up and looked at him, wondering how he was always so good at reading me.

"You were about to get up and suddenly froze like you were paralyzed and couldn't move," he explained.

"I was going to go clean up, but then I felt, you know—*the stuff*—and I realized that maybe I shouldn't do that right away. You know, if we're really trying to make a ba…" my voice trailed off as fear stopped me from finishing the sentence.

"A baby?" he finished for me. "We were definitely trying to make a baby, Abby. You don't have to be afraid to talk to me about it."

"I know," I laughed nervously. "But I didn't expect everything to happen right away. I mean, I don't regret it—

at all—but I guess I'm just used to being prepared for stuff, so now I don't know what to do, and you're here in my bed watching me, so now it feels even more weird."

"Okay," he said and popped up off of the bed.

I expected him to get dressed and leave, but instead, he grabbed a few pillows and scooted off the bed.

"Lift your butt," he instructed as he stood in front of me and waited.

"What?" I propped myself up on my elbows and titled my head.

"Your butt—lift it so I can stick these pillows underneath you."

"Why?"

"To keep my swimmers swimming. Now lift."

I fell back on the bed laughing and lifted my hips and butt. His fingers skimmed my skin as they adjusted the pillows beneath me.

"There, that should do it," he said with his hands on his hips while he admired his work.

I felt silly laying on the bed with my vagina lifted toward the ceiling, but the angle did seem to help make sure nothing leaked out. Maybe he had a point.

"How long do you propose that I stay this way?" I asked, looking over at him as he laid down beside me again.

He made no effort to get dressed, his ridiculously gorgeous body on full display, including his dick lying comfortably on his stomach.

"I don't know, maybe ten or fifteen minutes?"

"Is that a scientific answer?" I teased.

"No, but I did the math in my head. That's how I got that answer."

"The math?"

"Yeah. I can swim laps for about ten minutes before I get tired, so I figure that my swimmers can probably go the same amount of time—give or take. I think fifteen minutes would be a safer bet."

I closed my eyes and laughed.

"I think you're taking this whole *swimming* thing a little too literal."

"Nope, it's true. They're going to swim up your vagina and then merge onto the fallopian tube express before making their final stop at the uterus where they'll turn into little tadpoles and continue swimming around in your womb."

I covered my face and tried to hide the blush.

"Okay—first of all—I think you have a few details about that process wrong. Second—I don't think I'm ready to hear *you* say vagina or uterus." I shivered as a chill spread through my naked body.

Suddenly I felt his warm hand on mine as he pulled it away from my face.

"Would you rather that I say pussy," he asked, his tone a notch lower than before.

My breath hitched in my throat as I felt his eyes roam across my body, but for once, I didn't feel the urge to hide it.

"Because your *pussy* is quite beautiful, and I can't help but wonder what it tastes like."

I tried to speak, but the words wouldn't come out. My chest rose and fell heavily as his fingers trailed across my skin, leaving goosebumps in the wake.

He rolled over, holding my hips in his hands as he placed delicate kisses along my stomach.

"Can I taste you, Abby?"

His mouth was hovering right above my wetness, waiting for my permission. I felt the ache build between my legs and knew that I was ready for more with him.

"Mmhmm," I moaned, digging my fingers into his hair.

"Say it," he commanded, his tongue tickling the skin right above my clit.

"Yes, Nate," I cried out as he slid a finger inside me. "Taste me."

He growled out before lowering his mouth over my pussy and sliding his tongue through my part. I bucked off the bed, the sensation too much for me when his hands gripped my hips and held me down again.

I closed my eyes and let my legs fall open as he made himself at home in between them, delivering the most delicious torture I had ever felt before. A few minutes later, my body trembled around him as another orgasm ripped through me and left me seeing stars.

Nate Wilson had been many things to me over the years, but tonight, he was orgasm giver extraordinaire.

Six
Abby

"Why are you moving so funny this morning?" Jane asked as she studied me over the glass display I had just filled with this morning's pastries.

"I'm not," I said, ignoring her as I added a few more bagels to the other side and closed the door. I set the tongs down on the counter and looked up to find her light brown eyes narrowed and fixated on me.

"Yes you are. You're like…." She moved her body in weird circles as if trying to imitate me and then said, "super loose. Not all tight and rigid like you usually are."

I raised an eyebrow and planted my hands on my hips.

"I'm rigid?" I asked in disbelief.

"No, not per se," she laughed. "I've just never seen you look this… relaxed."

I shrugged and looked away, hoping that someone would come in looking for their daily caffeine fix so I could avoid the conversation that I knew was about to happen. Jane was only a year older than me, but she probably knew me better than anyone—aside from Nate.

"Oh. My. God!" she exclaimed, pulling my attention back to her. She clasped her hands over her mouth as her face lit up and her eyes widened. "You totally did it, didn't you?"

The heat prickled my skin along my neck as the blush spread across it. I quickly tried to rub it away with my hand, only making it worse.

"I don't know what you're talking about," I mumbled, looking around desperately for help.

"Yes you do. You totally *did it!*"

The seconds ticked by at an annoyingly slow pace while she put all of the pieces together.

"You're relaxed like you've been fucked senseless and blushing nonstop, which proves that you did it!" She squealed and clapped her hands while bouncing excitedly. "How was it?"

"I'm not going to tell you that," I blurted out, putting a hand over my heart protectively. My night with Nate had been fantastic, and she was right—I had been fucked senseless. But I wasn't about to divulge the dirty details with her.

"So it did happen! I knew it!" She spun around in a circle, pointing her fingers in the air as she did a celebratory dance.

"It's not what you think," I lied, leaning back against the counter behind me. I felt somewhat hidden by the glass cases of pastries that separated us, but I knew it wasn't enough.

"So you didn't have sex with your best friend—who is *hot as fuck*—and maybe forgot to use a condom so you could *accidentally* have his baby and create the life that you've dreamed about since you were a little girl?"

I blew out a breath and forced my hair to fly across my face.

I hung my head and tried to think of how much to tell her. Out of everything that Nate and I had discussed, we hadn't talked about how we would handle things from here out. Did we tell people about us? Were we an *us?* Were we still just best friends that now banged to make other people? There was so much we needed to go over, and I didn't want to be disrespectful to him by talking to my sister about it first.

"Okay, so maybe it is what you think it is," I said quietly, looking around to make sure no one could overhear us—not that anyone else was here. But still.

"Abby! This is amazing! Why are you being so weird about it?" she asked, pulling my arm and tugging me out from behind the counter.

I followed her over to a table and sat down.

"I don't know," I sighed, resting my hands in front of me. "I guess I just haven't processed everything yet. It all happened so quickly."

"Oh my God," she replied, frowning and making a disgusted face. "Like he's two-pump chump?"

"No! Jane!" I laughed, shaking my head.

"You said it happened quickly." She shrugged and leaned back against her chair, sipping her latte.

"I meant the whole 'us crossing the line' thing, not the actual sex part."

"So, was the sex good at least?"

She raised her eyebrows and smiled as she waited for the details she desperately wanted.

"It was… fantastic. Mind-blowing. Unlike anything I've ever had before."

"Even with Colin?"

I nodded.

Colin was my high school sweetheart, and the whole town expected us to get married and have babies right after graduation. While I was on board with that idea, Colin got a football scholarship that allowed him to move out of state and chase a different dream.

I had been with a handful of guys after Colin, but they were all lackluster, so I always assumed Colin was just amazing in bed. It turned out that after a few minutes with Nate last night, Colin was really just as bad as the others that I had been with.

It wasn't necessarily that he didn't know what he was doing, but he was like all of the other guys I had been with who were more focused on their own pleasure that they didn't put much effort into mine. I knew that it was frustrating to spend that much time trying to get someone off, so I never bothered to ask for anything from anyone. It was as simple as a quick fuck, and then I would take care of myself with my magical little bunny once I was by myself.

But after last night with Nate, I couldn't imagine ever going back to that damn rabbit. Nate was skilled and patient and attentive. All of the things that none of the other guys had ever been. He didn't struggle to get me to orgasm, nor did he rush through it just so he could get his. There was even the additional one that he gave me when he asked to go down on me and didn't want anything in return. That still blew my mind and I felt my legs clench at the memory of

Nate's soft hair tickling the inside of my thighs.

"It must have been really amazing," Jane commented, pointing a finger at me. "I've never seen you this distracted by something before in my life."

I lifted my hands and covered my face.

"What am I even doing? This is crazy—all of it is so crazy!"

"It's not crazy," she laughed. "It's fun and you're single, so why not do it?"

"It was fun," I giggled, wiggling my toes in my flip-flops.

"Are you going to do it again? Does he have a huge dick?" She snuck in the last question quickly, earning another raised brow from me.

"I don't know. We didn't really talk about that," I answered, deciding to ignore her second question. Nate didn't just have a huge dick—he had a monster-sized dick that required me to take some Advil this morning after sitting on an ice pack after he left last night.

"What did you talk about?"

"Just the basic idea of it. I was mumbling and rambling on about it, and he volunteered to do it."

"You didn't ask him directly?"

I shook my head and scrunched my face.

"So he just volunteered to be your baby daddy?"

"In a way," I laughed. "But he could tell that I was hinting at it being him."

"He's always been able to read you like a book." She smiled, and I felt it in my heart—my older sister's approval of my unconventional approach to starting a family.

We sat there quietly for a few minutes.

"So, what if it doesn't happen the first time? Do you think he would be on board with doing it again?"

"I don't know. We both agreed that it would be just one time."

"But you didn't talk about it."

"Nope."

"Well, do you know where you're at in your cycle? Are you ovulating?"

I gave her a blank stare and tried to remember when my last period was.

"I have no idea."

"You don't keep track of your periods?" she asked in disbelief.

"Why would I? I haven't been with anyone, so I didn't need to worry about it. It just comes, does its thing, I eat a lot of chocolate, and then move on with my life."

"Abbbyyyy," she groaned. "You should still keep track of it. It could be an indication of a number of health-related issues."

"You sound like mom," I muttered. "Why do we have so many doctors in the family?"

"Well, she's right about that one, but that's beside the point now. Do you have a general idea of when you might have had your period? Was it before your birthday?"

"I don't know, Jane," I whined. "That whole week was like a black hole of depression. I don't remember anything that happened during it."

"Come on, it wasn't that bad."

"Now you sound like Nate," I laughed. "He cooked me dinner for my birthday last night."

"And then gave you the best sex of your life. Ugh, I'm so jealous of you. You always get the best birthday gifts," she teased.

"Well, he did give me *two* orgasms, so yeah, I guess that was the best gift I could get."

"Alright, well, now I'm just downright depressed." She laughed and stood up. "I have to get going, but try to see if you can remember when you had your period. I can help you calculate ovulation, but I'll need that first."

"I'll do my best."

I stood up and hugged her, already feeling different, as if my life had changed in a way I had never seen coming.

Seven
Nate

"You look tired," Rodriguez commented as he slid down on the barstool next to me and spun his bowl of oatmeal around on the counter.

"I am."

"I told you, it's all downhill after you turn forty," Capshaw laughed from the stove.

I peered at him over my coffee mug but didn't respond as I took a sip. The guys were used to busting my balls. We were the only fire station in Beaumont Creek and rarely saw any action, which left plenty of time for us to get on each other's nerves out of boredom.

But the fact was that I was tired from staying up late at Abby's house last night. I knew that I should have gone home, but when she curled into me on the bed and fell asleep, I found it hard to leave her. I ended up crawling out of her bed around two this morning and locked up behind me before I went home to catch a few hours of sleep, which definitely wasn't going to be enough to get me through my forty-eight-hour shift.

We hadn't talked about what would happen after we had sex, so I wasn't about to tell anyone that I was tired from hanging out with her all night. It wasn't odd for us to spend almost all of our time together, but I didn't trust myself not to give anything else away with the stupid grin that felt plastered on my face every time I thought about her.

And I had done A LOT of thinking about her from the time I woke up this morning and couldn't stop. The way she moaned my name over and over or how her body reacted to my touch—those things would forever be engrained in my memory and were already creating problems with being able to focus on anything else today.

I stood up and pushed away from the counter, taking my coffee cup with me.

"I'm heading to my office. Rodriguez—you're on supplies duty, have your list to me by noon so I can put in the order. Capshaw, you're on rookie duty. Make sure you take some time to teach Jones how to cook without burning the damn station down."

"Yes, Captain," they said in unison as the rest of the guys tried to hide their laughter about Jones.

I knew we all had to start somewhere, but it had been a while since we had a rookie as clueless about cooking as Jones. But even the basics weren't that basic for him, and just last week, I had to stop him from sticking a potato wrapped in aluminum foil in the microwave. Before that, he almost burned the station down by forgetting to add sufficient water to his bowl of ramen noodles before popping them in the microwave. And the guys were still teasing him about the food poisoning fiasco a few months ago when everyone got sick after he used the same knife to cut the vegetables for the salad that he had used for raw chicken. I almost strangled him in between throwing up in the kitchen sink when he insisted that he had 'rinsed' them in between.

I plopped down at my desk and turned on my computer, making a note to order more sanitizing wipes. The day was just getting started, but I was already dreading this shift, knowing that I wouldn't get to see Abby for forty-eight hours until I was off again. It had never bothered me before, but after last night, I felt like I needed to see her again. Part of me wanted to check on her to make sure she was doing okay and didn't wake up regretting what had happened, but the other part of me wanted to take her in my arms and make love to her all over again. The problem was that there wouldn't be a next time because we both agreed that it would only be the one time.

By noon the guys had finished the basic chores around the station while I helped clean up the kitchen before Capshaw and Jones got back with the groceries. It was Rodriguez's birthday, so I asked Capshaw to pick up a cake while they were out and gave him some cash for it. While the guys drove me nuts most days, they were my brothers, and most of them had been working alongside me from when I started almost twenty years ago. Some had taken jobs elsewhere and had been promoted to Captain and Chief along the way, but I always stayed put and waited, knowing that someday the Captain position would be mine. I had a solid team and loved the guys who worked my shifts with me.

I used to think that I had everything I wanted in life until last night. Crossing that line with Abby had been life-changing, and now I imagined things that I never thought were possible before. *Babies. Wedding. A house filled with the smell of her baking and kids running around, chasing a dog.*

I shook my head and tried to clear it before heading into the kitchen with the guys. We sang happy birthday and then gathered around the table to bullshit with each other when my phone dinged with a text message.

Abby: How did he like the cake?

I smiled, knowing that out of everyone, Abby would remember that it was Rodriguez's birthday.

Me: He loved it. Said it's better than anything he's ever had before.

Abby: That's a lie.

Me: Nope, solid truth. He said he would divorce his wife to marry the woman who made it if she promised to make it for him every year for his birthday.

I was joking when I sent it, but damn if I didn't feel a bit of jealousy spike through me at the thought of Abby being with someone else.

Abby. Stop. It.

Abby: I'm going to tell Gwyn he said that.

Me: Eh, she would probably be willing to let him go if he promised her a slice of cake.

Abby: It's not that special—it's just a cake!

Me: You don't give yourself enough credit, Abs. You make delicious cakes, and they're all that everyone in Beaumont Creek talks about.

She was quiet for a few minutes, and I could picture her smiling while staring at the text. I was disappointed that

I didn't go pick up the cake, but the guys were already going to be out running errands, and I didn't want to draw attention to myself by insisting that I go pick it up. It would have definitely perked up my day to get to see her. *Maybe give her a hug or two. Sit her up on the counter and lower myself between her legs while I ate her sweet pussy.*

My phone dinged again, pulling me out of my dirty daydream.

Abby: They have plenty more to talk about than my cakes. Like the drama between Kylie and Paul.

Me: I haven't heard. Can't say that I care to either.

Abby: Same ol' gossip.

Me: How's your day going?

Abby: It's good. Quiet.

Me: There's something you're not telling me.

Abby: …..

Abby: …..

I felt the corners of my lips tug upward as I waited for her to finish typing whatever it was that she kept writing and deleting as the dots bounced on the screen.

Abby: No there's not.

Me: We both know better than that. Spill it.

I knew Abby better than she knew herself, so it was needless to say that I could call her bullshit when I saw it. Abby was by nature a talker—even in her text messages. The only time that she was quiet or her text messages were short was when she was avoiding something.

Abby: Jane stopped by this morning.

I frowned, unsure of why that would be something she hid from me. She was close to her sister and they talked almost every day. It wasn't unusual that she would stop in to grab her daily coffee before heading to work. She was a single mom with two adorable kids and Beaumont's favorite pediatrician. Okay—so she was the *only* pediatrician, but she was really great with kids, and everyone loved her.

Me: Is everything okay with her?

Abby: She's fine. She's.... overly excited?

Me: About what?

Abby: She guessed what happened.

It took a few seconds for it to finally make sense and for me to understand what she was talking about. Her sister knew that we had sex.

Eight
Abby

I hadn't talked to Nate much while he was on shift, and I couldn't help but wonder if he was feeling weird about Jane knowing that we had sex. I didn't mean to freak him out or embarrass him, it just happened, and I wanted him to hear it from me and not from her if, for some reason, he ran into her before I told him. It was unlikely that they would see each other, but stranger things had happened.

I was getting ready to close for the day, thankful that I had the next couple of days off. I used to work seven days straight until Nate convinced me to hire someone that I could trust to run things when I wasn't there. Sherry worked for me for over a year before I offered her a promotion and made her the assistant manager. We worked every other weekend, allowing each other to have a full weekend off so we didn't get burnt out, and this was my weekend off.

I locked up after the last customer left around four and was ready to get the hell out of there, go home, and drink a glass of wine. Then it occurred to me that I no longer had that luxury of just drinking whenever I wanted to because I had no idea if I might be pregnant. It had only been three days since we had sex so obviously I knew that things didn't move that fast, but I still didn't want to risk anything early on.

I stopped by the grocery store on my way home and grabbed a few essentials. Usually, Nate and I would make plans to hang out if we were both off on the weekend, but I had yet to hear from him. He finished his forty-eight-hour shift this morning and was likely just busy—not avoiding me like I had been obsessing over all day.

Deciding it was better to be over-prepared, I grabbed stuff to make dinner and added a six-pack of his favorite beer in case he came over. As I was checking out, my phone rang and I groaned when I saw my mom's name on the screen. I smiled at the clerk and waited for her to hand me my receipt before pushing my cart to the parking lot while holding my phone between my ear and shoulder.

"Hi, mom," I answered, trying to get hold of the cart as I went down the small hill toward my car. I hated that the parking lot was uneven and that no one ever thought to fix it.

"What are you doing? You sound like you're out of breath."

"I am," I huffed, jerking the cart hard to the right to turn it the other way.

"Were you blowing something?"

"Mom!"

"Well, just asking."

I rolled my eyes and stopped the cart at the back of my car, holding the bottom of it in place with my foot while I fumbled through my purse to find my keys.

"Aren't you going to ask why I'm calling?" she prodded.

I felt my neck tense as I tried not to drop the phone. Finally, I found my keys and pulled them out, unlocking the car so I could start unloading the groceries.

"Why are you calling, mom?" I asked in my most condescending voice.

"Because I found you a date!" she squealed so loud that I pulled my head away, and the phone fell to the ground. I grumbled and picked it up.

"Mom, I don't need you to find me a date."

"Of course you do. If not, you'd be getting them on your own."

"How do you know that I don't get my own dates?"

"Because everyone around town would be talking if you did."

I rolled my eyes knowing that was true.

"Still, I don't need you meddling in my life and trying to set me up. No offense, but you have terrible taste in men when it comes to picking them for me."

"I do not," she scoffed, sounding genuinely offended.

"When was the last time you tried to set me up with someone decent?" I asked, hand planted firmly on my hip even though she couldn't see it.

"Mr. Bucky wasn't that bad," she said quietly.

"MOM! He's sixty years old and walks with a cane. He has grandkids my age!"

"He's a nice man and was really excited to take you to dinner."

"For the early bird special, mom. He also had a buy one, get one free coupon."

"See, he's frugal and good with his money."

"You're impossible," I muttered, shaking my head. I loaded the last few bags of groceries into the trunk and then shut it.

"So do you want to hear about this guy or not?" she asked, more irritated now.

"Not really. But I know I'm going to anyway, so we may as well get on with it."

"You know, you're never going to land a man with that kind of attitude."

I bit my tongue and kept from saying what I really wanted to say. She wasn't going to listen anyway. The only truth she cared about was the one she harbored in her mind, and anything else was simply a lie.

"Anyway," she continued, "I met the nicest man today down at the harbor. He's new to town and is excited to take you to dinner on Tuesday!"

"What?!" I blurted out, my eyes nearly bulging out of my head. "Mom, you cannot set dates for me."

"Why not?"

"Because it's incredibly rude. You don't know if I'll even like this guy, and I actually have to work that day."

"I know, dear. I already checked your schedule. He's going to meet you there. You won't have to go far, and Sherry will be there if you need anything."

"So he's taking me to dinner at *my* café. The one that I own."

"Don't be so dramatic about it. It's a chance for you two to sit down and talk, see if there's something there. If it doesn't work out, no one loses out on anything."

I tried to take a slow and steady breath to calm myself, but it was impossible. My blood was boiling, and even though I should have expected it from her, I still couldn't believe she had done this.

"It's just one date, Abby. Dinner with a nice man. It won't kill you to do this for me."

"You do hear how ridiculous you sound, right?"

"I would watch how you talk to me, *Abby.* Men don't like women with smart mouths."

"No, mom. They like them with big ones so they can take their co—"

"Oooh, you're gonna hear about that later," Nate whispered in my ear, startling me.

I spun around, hand clutched to my chest as I stared at him.

"Mom, I gotta go." I didn't wait for her to say anything more before I hung up and tucked my phone into my pocket.

"Hey," I said a little too breathlessly as my eyes scanned over his body and how muscular it looked beneath his simple t-shirt that clung in all of the right places. My fingers itched to reach out and touch him. To feel the ripples that I knew were hiding beneath the thin layer of fabric. "What are you doing here?"

He looked down at his shopping cart and patted the handle. "Just stopped to grab some groceries for the weekend. You?"

"Same."

"What's up with your mom?" he asked as we walked the few steps to his truck.

"She set me up on another date," I said absently while I watched him lean into the back seat to set the bags on the floor. His shirt raised slightly, showing the black ink of the tattoo that went down the side of his torso.

"With who?"

"Some new guy in town." I looked up and met his eyes, noticing the slight smirk playing at the corner of his mouth. He caught me checking him out, and he knew it.

"You going?"

"I don't have much of a choice. Apparently, she called and got my schedule from Sherry and arranged for him to meet me at the café on Tuesday."

"He's taking you to dinner at your own café?" His brow arched in disbelief.

"Yup."

"Wow. And I thought it was bad that she was trying to set you up with the old guy with the senior discount." He whistled through his teeth and shook his head.

"I'll figure out a way to get out of it. I just don't feel like dealing with her right now."

He nodded and closed the truck door before taking his shopping cart back.

"So, what are you up to now?" he asked.

"Nothing. I was heading home. No big plans."

"Want to come over, and I'll make dinner? We can watch a movie if you want?"

I felt my stomach summersault at the thought of being alone in Nate's house. It wasn't like I didn't spend almost all of my free time with him before, but now, things felt different.

"That sounds great. What do you want me to bring?"

"Just yourself. I've got everything covered." He winked, and I felt it melt my panties. Okay—maybe that was a bit dramatic—but they were suddenly feeling hotter than they were a few seconds ago.

"Okay," I stammered. "I'll drop my stuff off at home real quick, then head over."

"Can't wait."

He walked me the few steps back to my car and waited for me to get in before closing the door and giving me a quick nod. Keeping the lines clear between us was going to be harder than I thought.

Nine
Nate

I rubbed my hands over the cold cucumber in my hand to wash it while trying to avoid Abby's eyes as she watched me. It was ridiculous how flustered I felt washing vegetables, but now that I had slept with Abby, everything reminded me of sex. It was like I was a horny teenager again with nothing but sex on the brain.

"Are you washing it or trying to get it off?" she asked, interrupting my thoughts as my head whipped up to look at her. She nodded at the cucumber, a knowing grin spread tightly across her face as I gripped it the same way I would hold my dick.

"It's all your fault," I muttered low enough that she couldn't hear me. I finished washing the damn cucumber and turned the water off.

"Are you sure that you don't need help?" she asked, tipping her barstool forward as she leaned against the counter with her breasts pushing up over the top of her low-cut shirt. I forced myself to look away after taking one last glance and turned to grab the other vegetables.

"I'm good, thanks. It's just salad."

"Okay," she sing-songed, planting her butt back down on the barstool. "But I do know how to wash vegetables, and you have pasta that needs your attention."

I looked over at the pot of boiling water on the stove and groaned. She was right. I was beyond distracted, and she knew it.

"Alright," I sighed. "You're on carrot duty but don't go getting any ideas." I waggled the bunch of carrots at her as she giggled and took them to the sink to wash.

I turned my focus to the pasta and stirred the boiling noodles before checking on the sauce. It smelled amazing but a quick taste test would confirm if I had gotten it right. I lowered the spoon into the pot and then blew on it before bringing it to my lips. They parted slowly, my tongue sliding through to taste it when I found Abby's eyes on me.

I took my time pushing the spoon into my mouth while my eyes stayed locked on hers. When I pulled it out, I made sure she saw the way my lips wrapped around it and how my tongue licked up the last bit of sauce from the spoon.

She was as flustered as I was when she dropped the carrots and cussed before turning around and washing them again. We both stayed at our designated stations until dinner was ready. Everything smelled delicious as I pulled the garlic bread and chicken out of the oven. Abby had set the table while I was finishing up and made a spot for the rest of the food.

I joined her and sat down, debating whether to offer her a glass of wine. It's what I would usually do, but now that she was trying to get pregnant—and might already be—I didn't know if she would want to chance it.

"Do you want something to drink?" I asked, getting up to head back into the kitchen.

"Water is fine," she answered with a smile.

I went to the fridge and pulled out the surprise I had picked up while at the store earlier. I knew that Abby would likely be watching what she ate and drank from here on, and I wanted to make it easier for her to make the switch from her daily coffee and wine diet that she lived on.

Once everything was ready, I joined her at the table, sliding a glass of chocolate milk with a twisty straw in front of her.

"What's this?" she asked with a huge smile as she twirled the straw around.

"Chocolate milk," I answered with a shrug, as if it was no big deal.

"Nate," she sighed, touching her heart. "You didn't have to get me chocolate milk."

"It's not just for you, I'm having some too." I lifted my glass to show her.

She shook her head and laughed, bringing the straw to her lips to take a sip.

"Thank you."

I smiled and took a drink, feeling my heart swell with how happy she was over such a simple gesture. I knew that Abby loved chocolate milk, but her mom harped on her when she was growing up, lecturing her about all of the extra calories and how she should be eating her calories and not drinking them. On occasion, I would sneak a couple of packs of *YooHoo* over to her house, and we would sit on a blanket on the grass and watch for shooting stars while hiding from her mom.

We ate our food, hardly taking the time to talk because we were both too hungry. I was mid-bite when I looked up to find Abby with a breadstick in her hand, popping the last piece into her mouth. She then slowly licked her fingers and that was my undoing.

 "Damn it!" I shouted, slamming my fists on the table.

She looked up at me, panic on her face as she struggled to figure out what was wrong.

Heat flushed my face, embarrassed about my outburst and more so that I felt so out of control around her. My dick was constantly hard and throbbing, and my balls felt like they were ready to explode at any minute. It wasn't her fault but damn if I couldn't be around her without wanting to plant more of my seeds inside her. She was like a fucking garden I wanted to grow.

"What's wrong?" she asked, reaching forward to hold my hand.

I looked down at it, feeling the heat that blazed through me from the contact. Her skin was soft and warm, and I wanted to feel more of it. All of it.

"Nothing," I lied, forcing my voice to come out around the lump in my throat. "Sorry about that."

"It's not nothing. I can tell you're wound up about something."

My hand stayed rigid under hers, afraid to move because I didn't trust that I wouldn't reach out and pull her across the table and fuck her right then and there. We agreed that it would be just one time but my body was having a hard time honoring that.

"Nate?"

I looked up and found her eyes locked on mine. She squeezed my hand, encouraging me to tell her.

"I can't, Abby."

She slowly pulled her hand away and folded them in her lap under the table. Her eyes lowered and I could see the rejection quickly settling on her face.

Fuck! That's not what I meant to do. Nothing was going how I wanted it to and it felt like everything I tried to say was going to come out the wrong way.

"I know that we agreed that we wouldn't let this ruin our friendship," she started, then paused to take a breath. Her shoulders pulled back and she lifted her head to look at me. "I'm sorry that I crossed that line, and I know that we can't take it back, but I really don't want to lose you. We can try to pretend that it never happened, but if I'm…."

Her words fell short, dying in the air around us.

"Abby," I leaned forward and waited for her to look at me again. "I don't regret what happened. And if you are pregnant, we'll both be happy and excited about it."

I watched as some of the tension eased from her shoulders.

"Okay, then, what's wrong?"

I tilted my head back and ran a hand across the hair that dotted my jawline.

"Nothing's wrong. I'm just frustrated, that's all."

"About what?"

"Do you really want to know?" I asked, challenging her with the look in my eyes.

She nodded.

"I'm frustrated that all I want to do when I'm around you is fuck you senseless. I haven't been able to stop thinking about you and all of the ways I want to take you and how good it sounds to hear you moan my name as you come. My dick is constantly hard, begging for me to let it inside of you. I've snuck into my office and jacked off more in the past forty-eight hours than I have in my entire life. It's like you're a drug I'm addicted to, Abby. And I promised you that it would be just the one time, so I'm frustrated that I have to keep that promise because fuck if I don't want to bend you over this table and plow into you after watching you take that breadstick into your mouth like some prize-winning cock."

Ten
Abby

If someone would have told me that a woman could leap across the room in one single motion, I wouldn't have believed them. But that's exactly what just happened and how I ended up straddling Nate and knocking his bowl of pasta to the floor.

I had no idea what came over me but hearing him talk like that sent something straight through to my core, and suddenly, I was pouncing on my best friend and trying to dry hump him to get the relief that I suddenly needed.

"Abby," he groaned as I kissed the side of his neck, slowly gliding my tongue in circles around his ear.

I pushed myself harder against his groin, pleased when I felt his erection pressing against his jeans.

"Let's go to your bedroom," I offered as I scratched my nails up his chest, feeling his muscular chest under my fingers.

"Fuck it," he breathed before standing up and grabbing my ass to hold me against him as he walked us to the bedroom. "Just one time, my ass."

I laughed as he plopped me onto his bed and reached behind his head to pull his t-shirt off. He watched me hungrily as he stepped out of his jeans and tossed his briefs to the side. I was still fully dressed, enjoying the strip tease in front of me.

"I need you naked," he said, stopping in front of the bed and scanning his eyes over my body.

I grinned and undid my shorts before lifting my butt and pushing them down my legs before kicking them to the floor.

"That's better." He licked his lips and pulled my white lace panties off. "I kinda expected to see Friday on them," he laughed.

"I haven't worn days of the week underwear since I was seven," I snorted, laughing at the memory. "And I still hate stupid Andrew for showing the entire class on the playground. That was so embarrassing."

"I didn't mind."

I rolled my eyes and looked away as his fingers gently skimmed up between my thighs and slid into my folds. A soft gasp escaped while I closed my eyes and let my legs fall to the sides to let him in.

"I've missed her," he said softly, pumping two fingers in and out. "I'm happy to see that she missed me too."

"So much," I whimpered. I was wet and ready, the tease of his fingers against my clit almost too much to take.

I could feel the heat of his gaze on me but kept my eyes closed as I savored the moment. His lips trailed kisses across my stomach before dipping lower. The warmth of his tongue as it caressed my clit made me moan. I needed more of him and wrapped my fingers in his hair, holding his head firmly between my legs.

I hadn't gotten around to taking off my shirt, so I pulled it down as well as my bra, letting my breasts sit on full display. He sucked my clit as his fingers pumped harder inside of me. I rolled my nipples between my fingers, pulling hard enough to build my orgasm, and before I knew it, I was coming against his mouth. He continued his delicious torture, sucking every last tremor out of me.

Once I was done, he stood up and wiped his mouth before climbing up the bed and hovering above me. I was about to pull my bra back up when he leaned down and pulled a nipple into his mouth, feasting on it as if he hadn't eaten in days.

I groaned more, digging my fingers into his hair and arching my back off the bed. My orgasm was intense and felt amazing, but it didn't satisfy the need I had to have him inside of me.

My hand reached between us, grabbed his hard cock, and stroked him eagerly. I could feel his body tighten against mine and knew he wanted this as much as I did.

Suddenly he popped my nipple free and pulled back to watch my hand slide up and down his length.

"Fuck, Abby," he breathed. "How do you want it?"

It's not like I hadn't been obsessing over this since the last time I saw him, so I knew exactly what I wanted. Playfully I reached up and pushed him to his back before climbing on top. His dick jutted out, a drop of precum on the tip.

I wanted to sink down on top of him, but before I could stop myself, I was sliding down his body and taking him into my mouth. My eyes focused on his as he watched me take him all the way in, his cock touching the back of my throat. I relaxed my jaw and pushed him in further, loving the way his face looked as he watched. His hands wrapped down into my short hair and held on as I started bobbing my head and sucking him with hollow cheeks.

He grunted a few times, the muscles in his thighs super tight as he fought coming in my mouth.

"I need to fuck you, Abby," he groaned. "I don't want to come in your mouth, so you better stop."

I pulled back slowly, allowing him to pop out of my mouth. Seconds later, I was straddling him and sinking down onto the beast as he stretched me in the best possible way.

"Fuuucccckkkk," I cried out, tossing my head back and closing my eyes. His hands roamed my chest, tugging at my nipples before pulling them into his mouth and sucking while he allowed me time to adjust to his size.

I started rocking slowly, grinding my hips down until I found the perfect pace. He lowered his hands to my hips to guide me as his tongue continued to flick my hard nipples. The pressure build-up was insane, and I loved being in control as I rode him. Soon I had completely adjusted to him and leaned back with my hands on the sides of his thighs as I bounced hard on his thick cock.

My breasts jiggled in time with my movements, making me feel like the girls in the porno videos I had watched when I needed to get off. For a moment, I thought about what it would be like to record us having sex and watch it later. Would there be a next time? I didn't know. There wasn't even supposed to be this time, but here we were.

I felt him tense beneath me and knew that he was getting

close. I leaned forward as he reached for me and let him guide my hips as I rode him harder and faster. Thanks to Nate, my body was now in a slightly tilted position that allowed me to feel the friction against my clit as we fucked. I knew that I was getting closer to having another orgasm by the way my spine tingled and my nipples hardened even more. As if reading my body, Nate pulled a nipple into his mouth and sucked hard as he came at the same time.

Once we were done, I climbed off and rolled onto the bed beside him. I was totally and completely spent, trying to catch my breath. My eyes fluttered closed as I stayed in this blissful state of being thoroughly fucked when I felt Nate's hands on my thighs as he tucked another pillow under me. I laughed and lifted my butt, thankful that he was being so thoughtful.

He plopped down beside me, and we laid there for what felt like half an hour. Finally, he rolled over and looked at me.

"I didn't get to finish my pasta," he said, raising a brow at me.

"Sorry," I laughed. "You had me at breadstick, and I just couldn't control myself."

"Well, I was definitely right about that."

"About what?"

"That you suck a mean cock. Seriously, Abby, that mouth of yours…."

I bit my lower lip and pulled it between my teeth nervously.

"Where did you learn to do that?"

"I'm not telling you that," I squeaked, too afraid to tell him that I learned it by watching porn but had never tried it on anyone before tonight.

"Abby…"

"I'm not telling."

"If you say it was one of the losers you've dated…." He sighed heavily.

"Where else would I have learned it? It's not like I'm just setting up shop and blowing random guys in the parking lot."

He widened his eyes and tried to pull his lips into a thin line to avoid laughing.

"What? It's not!" I laughed and smacked my hand against his chest.

"Project Abby Blows," he chuckled, rolling to the side as I picked up a pillow and hit him with it.

"You fucker," I muttered, tempted to hold the pillow over his face for a few minutes.

"Don't even think about it," he teased.

"About what?" I acted innocent and pretended like I hadn't been thinking about it.

"Smothering me with the damn pillow."

"How the hell do you do that?"

"I know what your're thinking before you even think it."

"I highly doubt it."

"Trust me, Abby, I know more about you than you will ever know."

"Oh yeah?" I asked, feeling brave. "Like what?"

He got up and picked his clothes up from the floor, pulling his jeans on and hiding my favorite part of him: his cock.

"That you watch porn to get off."

My jaw dropped as I sat up and stared at him, totally forgetting that the girls were still hanging out. His eyes slowly trailed down before I snapped and pulled my bra and tank top back up.

"I do not!"

"Don't be embarrassed about it," he said with a shrug. "Porn can be fun. Maybe we can watch it together."

I didn't say anything, I just sat there staring at him in disbelief as he pulled his t-shirt over his head.

"Oh, and Abby?"

"Yeah?" My voice was quiet and nearly stuck in my now dry throat.

"If you ever try to smother me with something, I prefer it to be your pussy as you sit on my face and let me eat you out."

And just like that, he was gone, and I was left sitting there with that image to think about.

Eleven
Nate

I rolled over and slung my arm over Abby, wondering why she was so soft and squishy. Forcing my eyes open, I looked over and found her side of the bed empty and one of the pillows pushed beside me in her place. I scrubbed a hand down my face and then got out of bed to go look for her.

It wasn't like her to leave without telling me, so I was pretty confident that I would find her in either the bathroom or the kitchen. Last night had been a late night after we both agreed that it wasn't just one time after all and kept fucking throughout the night. Her body was like a wonderland, and I was determined to make every inch of it mine.

I pulled on a pair of sweats and made a quick pit stop in the bathroom to relieve myself before heading to the kitchen. As predicted, I found her at the stove wearing nothing but one of my *Foo Fighters* t-shirts that barely covered her naked ass as the smell of bacon floated in the air around us.

Casually, I slipped up behind her and wrapped my hands around her waist as I kissed the back of her neck. I loved how cute her short hair looked on her, but I loved it even more that I had easy access to kiss her in the spots that I knew turned her on without trying.

"Good morning to you, too," she giggled, letting her head tilt to the side to give me access.

"It's a great morning seeing you stand in my kitchen, wearing my shirt and no fucking panties."

"How do you know I don't have panties on?"

I let my hand slide from her waist down to her hip before lifting the shirt and caressing her.

"It barely covers your ass to start with, and if I know you, you're not wearing any because you know what I want for breakfast."

"Bacon?" she replied coyly over her shoulder.

"More like a pussy sandwich."

Her cheeks flushed red, making my dick twitch in response. I loved how easily she flushed and that I could dirty-talk her as much as I wanted because even though she acted shocked at what I said, it always turned her on.

"You had that last night," she said quietly as she turned her attention back to the food in the skillet. I looked over her shoulder at the spread she was working on, and my stomach growled in anticipation.

"What can I say? It's my favorite."

"Well, you should probably eat some real food first."

"But you're saying there's a chance I can eat you again when we're done?"

I reached into the cupboard beside her head and grabbed a few plates, watching as she blushed and refused to look at me.

"Maybe," she mumbled under her breath.

I chuckled and got the rest of the stuff we needed while

she finished plating the food. We sat on the couch this time and watched a cooking show since there wasn't much on at eight in the morning on a Saturday.

Once we were done, I cleaned up and sent her to go shower. I might have rushed through the dishes and tossed stuff in the dishwasher that wasn't supposed to go in there- but knowing that she was wet and naked in my shower had my dick straining to get to her. It was like her pussy was a siren and my cock heard her call.

I tossed the towel on the counter and started stripping my clothes off as I rushed down the hall before she turned off the shower.

Thankfully she was still lathering the shampoo in her hair when I got there and didn't seem to mind as I opened the door and stepped inside to join her. Her body was amazing, and my fingers ached to reach out and touch her but I refrained, waiting for her to initiate it. The last thing I wanted was to come across as some sexually crazed deviant, even though that's how she had me feeling lately.

Her eyes were closed as she rinsed out the conditioner, the water gliding over her breasts and dripping down her body.

"I can feel you watching me," she said, slowly peeking one eye open.

"I can't help it," I admitted. "I have a naked woman in my shower with water running down her body. It's hard not to."

She smiled and closed her eyes again, letting her hands run down her neck and over her breasts.

"Are you touching yourself?" she asked, her voice slightly hoarser.

"I am now." I grabbed my cock, which was already hard, and stroked it, thinking about all of the different positions I could fuck her in the shower.

She opened her eyes and let them drift down to my hand. Her tongue slipped out and wet her lips as her fingers dipped down and disappeared between her legs.

We stayed there for a few minutes, watching each other masturbate before I couldn't take it any longer.

"I need to fuck you, Abby," I blurted out with new desperation in my voice.

"It's about fucking time," she replied, pulling her hand away as she took a few steps toward me and wrapped her arms around my neck. Her mouth crushed down on mine as she brought her legs up and locked onto my hips. I grabbed her ass and pinned her to the wall so she didn't fall, and then grabbed my dick and slid it inside of her.

"God, that feels so fucking good every time," she moaned and ground her hips.

Her mouth was back on mine, kissing me before I could respond. This time wasn't long and filled with foreplay— it was a quick fuck that both of us wanted and needed. Abby slipped a finger between us and rubbed her clit until she came on my dick. The way her pussy tightened and clenched around me was enough for me to shoot my load inside of her.

We finished and rinsed off before we got out and got dressed. It was barely after nine, and we were both off all weekend with no other plans than to fuck each other senseless, it seemed.

Twelve
Abby

"You didn't do anything *all* weekend?" Jane asked, eyeing me suspiciously over the top of her latte.

"I just hung out with Nate, like we always do."

I pulled a few pastries out of the display case and wrapped them in paper before adding them to the to-go box that I was getting ready for a call-in order. Mondays were always busy, and thankfully, today I was feeling alert and rested.

"Mmmhmm." She continued to eye me but didn't keep pushing. "So, are you excited about tomorrow?"

"What's going on tomorrow?" I asked, adding a few napkins to the bag before sealing it shut with a sticker.

"Your date, Abby. Remember?"

I closed my eyes and let my head fall back. *Fuck.*

"Ugh, I completely forgot about that," I muttered.

"I'm surprised mom hasn't called eighty times to remind you," she laughed.

"She's called me, but I was busy, so I didn't answer."

"Busy doing what?" she questioned with a knowing tone. "Possibly Nate?"

"Would you stop it with that?" I hissed, looking around the café to make sure no one had heard her.

She rolled her eyes and took a sip of her coffee.

"What are you going to do if you end up—*ya know*? Not tell everyone how it got there? Pretend that you don't know whose it is?"

"I haven't thought that far yet."

"Well, you better. Because if you two keep doing what I know you're doing—you're going to have some explaining to do whether you want to or not."

The front door opened, and the faint sound of a rooster crowing filled the room. I looked up and felt my heart skip a beat when I saw Nate walk in with a few guys from work. They were all in uniform since they started their shift this morning. It wasn't unusual for them to stop by and grab breakfast, but not knowing that he was coming had me feeling out of sorts.

I looked over to find a smug smile on Jane's lips as she stepped to the side so they could look into the display case.

"Hey guys," I said a little too breathlessly and with a forced smile. "Let me know what you want and I'll get your order started."

Nate gave me a look that made my knees weak, and I knew what he was saying that he wanted. I involuntarily pressed my legs together as if I was afraid that my vagina would willingly betray me and open up for him right here, right now, in front of everyone.

"I know what I want," Capshaw said, looking in Jane's direction as he made no effort to hide that he was checking her out.

She arched a brow and lowered her to-go cup from her mouth as she leaned against the wall.

When she didn't say anything, he kept pressing.

"What do you say, Jane? Wanna put me out of my misery and finally take me up on my offer?"

"Which one?" she snorted with an eye roll.

"Whichever one rocks your boat the most."

"Rocks my boat?"

He smiled and took a few steps closer to her. This now had the attention of the other guys, as well as a few of the regulars who had stopped by for breakfast. It was a casual crowd, and everyone already knew that Jane was about to put him in his place the way she always did.

"I've got the motion in the ocean, baby."

She let out a heavy sigh before turning and setting her cup on the short wall between us.

"When are you ever going to learn?" she asked, arms folded across her chest. She was dressed for work in a sleeveless silk shirt that buttoned down the front and tucked into the simple black A-line skirt that hugged her hips.

"Learn what?"

"That you need more than words to impress a woman. You talk *a lot* of shit but literally know nothing about women or what we really want."

"Ha," he scoffed. "I know what women want, and I make sure to give it to them every time."

"Oh yeah?" she challenged. "And what's that?" She cocked her head to the side and waited.

"Orgasms. Multiple."

"Have you ever given anyone one?"

"Hundreds of them."

He folded his arms over his chest to match her.

She pulled her lip between her teeth and worked it for a few seconds before taking a step closer to him and letting it pop free.

"Trust me, Capshaw. If you were giving women orgasms, you'd know. They'd be coming back for more. Not moaning and faking it so they could rush home to their trusty vibrator that never lets them down."

"They don't fake it."

"Wanna bet?"

He looked nervously over his shoulder at the guys watching with shit-eating grins on their faces. This wasn't going to end well for him.

"Did you know that when a woman has an orgasm, you can feel the walls of her vagina spasm? The more intense her orgasm is, the tighter she can clench around you as that orgasm rips through her. You can literally feel her coming."

His jaw dropped as he stared at her.

"Bullshit," he huffed out, shaking his head as if to clear the nonsense.

"I wish it was. It looks like you still have lots to learn." She turned and grabbed her cup off the wall and focused her attention on me. "I need to get going. Can I get a refill?"

"Of course." I tried to keep my laughter in, but I almost lost it when I looked up at Nate. He gave me a look that said that he knew exactly what she was talking about and that he could feel every time I came this weekend.

I worked on her latte and put the lid back on, too flustered to say anything else to her. She slid some money across the counter and darted out the door before I could fight with her about paying for her coffee. While the guys chatted about what to get, I put the cash in the register and took a sip of ice water, hoping it would cool me down.

"You okay?" Nate asked, standing off to the side and talking low so the guys didn't hear him.

"I'm good," I lied. "You?"

He licked his lips and rubbed them together before answering, "I'm good too."

I wanted to blurt out random responses like—*I know you are. You're the best I've ever had!* But I didn't. Instead, I tried to keep my focus on work but didn't realize how spaced out I was when Rodriguez was staring at me, waiting for me to answer his question.

"Abby?"

"I'm sorry, what?"

"I asked if you had any of that cake you made the other day? The one that just melts in your mouth?"

My heart was racing out of control as I watched Nate's face flush, remembering that I had made that cake this weekend and he ate it off of my naked body.

"Um, no. I don't have any. Sorry."

I felt like an idiot and knew they were growing suspicious as to why I was acting so strange.

"No worries, just thought I would ask," Rodriguez said before looking through the items in the other display cases.

Finally, they all made their selections and Sherry came out to help me get them ready. Nate was the last one to leave and lingered around for a few minutes until Sherry went back to the back.

"Are you sure you're okay?" he asked once we were alone.

I let out a heavy breath and shook my head.

"I don't know how to act around you in front of other people now," I admitted. "I feel like everyone knows what we've been doing because I'm acting like a complete fool."

"I don't think anyone knows," he shrugged. "Would it be terrible if they did?"

"No, I guess not. I just didn't know if we were telling anyone about—you know...."

"We don't have to tell them anything. But if they find out that we're fucking like bunnies, it wouldn't be such a terrible thing. At least I wouldn't have to worry about Jones checking you out anymore."

"He was not!" I laughed.

"Totally was. And trust me—between him and me—at least I can cook. Make good choices, Abby." He winked and tapped his knuckles on the counter.

"Trust me, I have no desire to do anything with Jones. I like a man that knows how to cook as good as he can fu—"

The door opened and the roosters crowed as a handful of people walked in.

"Saved by the bell," he whispered before giving me another panty-melting smile and walked out the door.

Thirteen
Nate

"So you're telling me that there is absolutely nothing going on with you and Abby?" Rodriguez asked as he stared at me from across the table.

I popped a piece of bagel into my mouth and chewed to keep it occupied so I didn't have to answer. I knew that I would get shit from the guys as soon as we got back to the station after they watched us together at her café.

While Abby tried—and failed desperately—to act normal, there was no way we could ever go back to the normal we used to have. Things were different now, and no matter how hard we tried, we couldn't uncross the line that we had already passed.

"There's definitely something going on," Capshaw snorted, then took a drink of water. "They were practically eye-fucking each other across the counter."

"At least I didn't get turned down," I countered, crumpling the paper the bagel was wrapped in and tossing it into the trashcan beside us.

"I didn't get turned down," he pouted. "It's just a game that we play."

"Are you sure you're both playing the same game?" I laughed and raised a brow at him.

"Jane likes me, but she's too afraid to let her guard down to show it. So it's easier to pretend that she can't stand me."

"Or maybe she just really doesn't like you," Rodriguez added.

"Very funny. Just wait and see; I'll get her to go on a date with me. Then she won't be able to stay away."

"One date with you and she'll probably leave town," I teased.

"So, back to you and Abby," Capshaw said, turning the attention back to me. "When did that start?"

"What are you referring to?"

"You know what we're talking about; there's no need to play dumb."

"Look," I said, pushing away from the table and standing over them. "Whatever's happening between Abby and me is between us. It's not anyone's business."

I walked to my office but didn't miss the whispered comments about how they knew something was going on. I closed the door and sat down, pushing a stack of papers to the side while I scrolled through pictures on my phone. There were random photos of the ocean and a few of me with the guys at the station, but the majority of them were Abby. Some of them while she posed and acted silly, and some of them she didn't know I had taken. Those were my favorite.

She was so beautiful and I couldn't stop staring at her beautiful brown eyes that stared up at me under thick lashes right after I had fucked her senseless last night. I don't know how long I kept her picture up, but the moment a text message popped up from her, I felt my cheeks burning from how tight my smile pulled across my face.

Abby: Do you want to do dinner tonight and maybe get food poisoning with me?

I frowned, wondering what she was up to.

Me: If you want sushi, I'll take you to a legit restaurant. We're not getting gas station sushi again.

Abby: It's not that. I'm supposed to have that date tomorrow night, and I need an excuse to get out of it.

Me: Why don't you just say no?

Abby: We both know that it's not that easy. I don't even know the guy's name or have his number. My mom set everything up and purposely kept all of the details from me so I couldn't cancel.

Me: What Rhonda wants, Rhonda gets.

Abby: It's so irritating.

Me: Why don't you just tell her you're already seeing someone?

Abby: She would never go for that. She would ask a million questions, and I wouldn't be able to keep my lies straight.

Me: Why do you have to lie?

Abby: Because I don't have a real boyfriend?

My stomach tightened as I thought about how to approach this with her. We hadn't agreed that this would be anything more than two friends who were fucking, but the thought of her going on a date with another man had me seeing red.

Me: But you could.

Abby: Who?

Was she really this naïve, or did she need me to spell it out for her? I thought it would be the obvious answer, given how we spent the entire weekend together, naked and in bed. Maybe I had read more into it than she did?

Abby: Someone's here. Gotta go.

I kept watching my phone, waiting for the bubbles to pop up on the screen to show that she was texting, but they never came. Irritated, I pushed my phone to the side and forced myself to get to work.

Fourteen
Abby

"I'm sorry, you're who?" My voice was awkwardly pitchy as I stared at the insanely attractive man in front of me who was shaking my flimsy hand that I somehow offered but didn't remember doing.

"Vince. Your mom told me you would be expecting me?" I hated the uncertainty in his voice and immediately felt angry at my mother for this little game she was playing.

"Sorry, I apologize about my reaction," I tried to explain. "She told me we were meeting tomorrow night."

"Ah, I see." He smiled, and the dimples in his cheeks winked at me.

Goodness, he was attractive. I tried to look past the tall, built frame that filled out the tailored suit he was wearing and focused on the ocean blue eyes that were watching me with curiosity.

"I can come back tomorrow if that's better?" he offered, forcing my eyes from his plump lips back to his eyes.

"Oh no, that's not necessary." I waved my hand and then saw the hurt look flash across his face when he thought I was blowing him off completely. "I mean, you're already here, and it's slow right now, so I can take a break if you'd like to sit down and have some breakfast?"

"That would be wonderful," he said, checking his watch. "My meeting isn't for another hour, so I'm all yours until then."

I smiled and did an awkward curtsy before darting through the employee-only door to the kitchen.

"I need help," I whispered to Sherry, who was adding the final touches to the cake she had baked this morning.

"What's wrong?" She looked concerned as she set the piping bag full of frosting on the counter.

"Is that the sex cake?" I asked, suddenly distracted.

"The what?"

"The *sex* cake."

"Abby, are you okay? Do you need to go home and lie down? I can call Nate—"

"No!" I blurted out, making her pull back. "We don't need to call Nate. I'm fine. Just a little flustered. The date my mom set me up with for tomorrow just showed up today because my mom is a dirty little rat that purposely told me the wrong day so I couldn't cancel."

"No shit! Is he good-looking?"

"Yes," I sighed, suddenly feeling guilty that I was swooning over another guy when I had just been in Nate's bed last night. "What am I doing?!"

"You mean besides your best friend?"

"Sherry!"

"Okay, sorry. I don't know, Abby. It can't be that bad, right? I mean, you can have coffee with him and see where things go. It's not like you have to strip down and fuck him on the counter."

"Sherry," I scolded again, feeling my cheeks burn red.

"What do you need help with?"

"Can you watch the front while I have a quick bite and coffee with him?"

"Of course, not a problem. I can finish the *sex* cake later."

I nodded and slipped off my apron, trying to feel braver than I was. Why was I so nervous, and worse, why did I feel so guilty still? She was right—it was just coffee and a pastry; we weren't going to go at it on the table. At the end of the day, Nate and I weren't in a relationship; we were just two friends who were having sex to make a baby. Nothing more than that. I needed to keep reminding myself of that simple fact—we were just friends. He probably didn't want anything more than that, so why shouldn't I have at least one date with the attractive stranger who made an effort to come meet me?

"Later, you'll have to tell me why we're calling this the *sex cake*." She nudged me with her elbow as she passed me and went to the front to help the new customer that was waiting.

I grabbed a few of the fresh danishes that I had baked this morning and joined Vince at the table in the corner.

"I'm going to get some coffee. Can I get you anything?"

"Coffee would be great, thank you."

"How do you take it?"

"Two cream and one sugar, please."

"You got it."

I smiled at a few of the regulars who had stopped in and felt a ping of jealousy when I found a couple of the women gawking at him and whispering about who he was. That was the problem with small towns—everyone was always in everyone's business.

I carried our coffee to the table and sat down across from him, thankful that I could look at the window and not the customers who were sure to be gossiping about this later.

He took a bite of the pastry and swiped his tongue across his lip to catch the crumbs.

"This is amazing," he said after wiping his mouth and swallowing the bite.

"Thank you."

"Did you make it?"

I nodded, taking a sip of my coffee.

"You're very talented. This is probably the best danish I've ever had."

My lips tugged upward at the compliment that rattled off his tongue so effortlessly.

"So, Vince, my mom said you're new to Beaumont Creek. What brings you here?"

"Work," he replied, lifting his mug to his lips. "I'm a financial planner. My office sent me here to work directly with a few of our clients."

"Where's home?"

"Cape May. Born and raised."

"Not too far from here," I commented, feeling the curious gazes sitting heavily on my back from the onlookers up front.

"What about you?"

"Beaumont Creek Girl, through and through."

He smiled and took another bite of his danish as I fidgeted under the table. We talked about random things for a few minutes until another customer walked in and the rooster crowed over our heads. I watched him try to fight his laughter at the atrocious sound and started laughing myself.

"That rooster has been making that same God-awful sound since I was a little girl and my grandparents owned this place."

"Are they still around?"

"No, they died ten years ago and left the Rockin' Rooster to me. I used to work here as a teenager, and once I started baking, I found that I didn't care to be anywhere besides the kitchen. It was a natural move for me to take it over, but I keep putting off replacing the damn Rooster."

"I think it's charming," he said with another dimple-filled smile.

I returned it and felt the tingling across my skin as I blushed.

We talked for half an hour, completely losing track of time when his phone dinged, and he groaned as he looked at it.

"I'm sorry," he sighed. "I better get going, or I'm going

to be late meeting my first client, and I'd hate to make a terrible first impression."

"No worries," I smiled, standing up to collect our trash.

"Would it be okay if I asked you to dinner sometime?" he asked, reaching for it before I could grab it. He tossed it in the trashcan by the door and then waited for my response with another beautiful grin.

"Sure, that would be nice."

I felt the heat flood my stomach with a combination of excitement and nerves. He seemed like a nice guy, and I found myself wanting to spend more time getting to know him. We exchanged phone numbers before he headed out the door, and I watched him leave, wondering why I felt like I had just stabbed my best friend in the back.

Fifteen
Nate

"How long do you need us there?" I jotted down the information on the notepad in front of me, almost relieved that I was being directed to lead my platoon to Ocean City to help provide mutual aid for a wildfire that had gotten out of control. It wasn't that I didn't want to stay in town and hang out with Abby, I just wasn't in the mood to hear any more about Vince.

She had texted me as soon as he left her work on Monday, letting me know that he was really nice and completely opposite of anyone her mom had ever set her up with before. She was so impressed by him that she had agreed to have dinner with him Thursday night. I had checked on her a few times last night, just to make sure she had made it home safe, but by eleven, she had told me they were back at her place and she would talk to me later.

I woke up cranky this morning, taking it out on the guys when we started our shift. It wasn't their fault, and thankfully they all knew me well enough to know that it wasn't personal and to give me space until I calmed down. I spent the better part of my morning working out and running on the treadmill to burn off the frustration that was still looming inside me.

No matter how hard I tried, I couldn't shake the nagging questions stuck on repeat in my head. *Did she like this guy? Did he kiss her goodnight? Did she let him? Did they do anything else?*

Thinking about Abby letting another man between her thighs had my blood boiling and I knew that I had no right to be upset about it. When we first started this thing between us, it wasn't to start a relationship with her. It was to get her pregnant. But damn if I didn't just cross that line but went so far over it that I would never be able to go back to seeing her as just a friend.

I had kicked myself repeatedly for not being man enough to tell her how I felt. There were plenty of opportunities, but I failed to take any of them. Then suddenly, some smooth-talking financial planner rolls into town, and now they're making plans of another kind.

My mood stayed sour until I got the phone call. As Captain, I could have sent one of the other platoons to go, but I wanted the break from Beaumont Creek. Okay, so I really wanted the break from Abby. Maybe if I went away for a few weeks, I could clear my head and come back with a better idea of what I wanted. Maybe I was just pussy drunk and couldn't think straight? Going to Ocean City was exactly what I needed.

I was busy with paperwork when I got a text message from Abby asking if I wanted to do dinner tonight. I quickly responded, letting her know I was on shift today and tomorrow so I couldn't. Had we been talking more, like we used to, she would probably know that. But then I reminded myself that she didn't do anything wrong by going on a date with someone she was interested in and that I was being childish.

She sent a sad face emoji and then apologized for not realizing that I was back on shift. She asked about next week instead, but I let her know that I would be gone for a few weeks.

Abby: So I'm not going to see you for three weeks?

Me: Sorry. It might be longer, it depends on how long they need us there to help with the fire and clean up after.

Abby: That sucks.

Me: You still have Vince. It's not like you'll be lonely. You won't even realize that I'm gone.

Abby: What's that supposed to mean?

I blew out an irritated breath and pushed my phone to the side. I was being a dick, and she was picking up on it.

Me: Nothing.

Abby: Bullshit.

Her messages were coming in as quickly as I was sending mine, which meant that she was laser-focused on our conversation right now and if I didn't talk to her, she was likely to Facetime me any second.

Abby: What's that supposed to mean?

Me: I didn't mean anything by it. We know you like Vince, it wasn't an insult.

Abby: Why wouldn't I know you were gone? Do you think he's going to replace you or something?

Me: I never said that.

Abby: You're acting like it.

Me: I'm just in a bad mood today.

Abby: Why are you in a bad mood? What happened?

I fell in love with my best friend while trying to get her pregnant, so she could have the life she always wanted then she turned around and met her real-life prince charming. That's what happened.

Me: Nothing happened. I'm just tired and need to get back to work.

It took a few minutes for her to respond, and I knew that she wasn't buying my lies at all. Finally, her last text message came through.

Abby: I'll let you get back to work. When you finally get your head out of your ass and want to talk, I'll be here.

Sixteen
Abby

It turned out that three weeks without Nate was longer than I imagined it would be. Vince and I had gone out a handful of times, but I found myself constantly thinking about Nate and whether he was safe in Ocean City. It didn't usually bother me when he would be called out to help fight wildfires, but this time was different, and I couldn't put my finger on why.

Maybe it was because I felt like things were weird between us when he left, or maybe it was because he hardly talked to me the entire time he was gone—which was extremely unusual for him. Even when he was out of town, he checked in several times and we would usually Facetime each other a handful of times while he was there. This time, his text messages were short and we didn't try to call each other once.

The sun was burning hot as I sat on the boat, trying to shield my face with the wide-brimmed sunhat I was wearing. I had already lathered the sunscreen on a handful of times, but it felt like my body was cooking from the inside out.

My parents always enjoyed getting out on the water for the Fourth of July, spending the day watching my dad get frustrated when he didn't catch anything, and then watching the fireworks in the sky at night. This time was no different other than instead of having Nate on the boat beside me drinking a beer, I had Vince chatting with my mother about stocks and bonds—things she had no clue about but pretended, nonetheless. I knew that I should be upset by the way she was blatantly flirting with him and even maybe a little jealous of the attention he was giving her, but I wasn't. And maybe that should have been more of a sign that I just wasn't feeling the chemistry with him the way I should have. If I was being honest with myself, it was nothing compared to what I felt when I was with Nate.

Jane and I sat at the back of the boat, trying to shade ourselves under the thin canopy flapping wildly in the wind while my dad cursed and reeled his line in from the front of the boat. My mom sat across from Vince, who was sitting in the driver's seat, looking more than comfortable as she shamelessly flirted with him. Why she was like that—I had no fucking idea, but I couldn't wait to tell Nate about it. *If* I ever talked to him again. It was a bit dramatic, but I was starting to get this nagging feeling that our friendship had shifted into something that I didn't like.

Vince handled my mother with respect while also keeping her at a distance. He would nod his head and listen as she carried on, but every few minutes, I would find him stealing glances and showing me that beautiful smile as if he couldn't wait to get away from her and spend some time with me.

The wind picked up and the water got choppy, forcing us to rock back and forth against the waves. I wasn't one who got motion sick easily, but suddenly the constant rocking had me feeling queasy. I looked around for a bucket or something to throw up in when Jane spotted me, her eyes wide with concern.

"Are you okay?" she asked quietly, trying not to draw any attention our way. I glanced at my mother, who was flipping her hair over her shoulder as she laughed carelessly, not at all focused on my dad or his struggle at the front of the boat.

"Yeah, the waves are making me a little nauseous."

"I'll grab a bucket," she offered, getting up and pulling the bottom of her bikini down to cover her cheeks. The kids were with their dad this weekend which meant she could wear her itsy-bitsy bikini without hearing about it from her over-controlling and jealous ex.

She shuffled around up front, picking up the extra life vests as she tried to find something for me to use. My dad uttered a loud curse word, pulling the rod back against his chest as he quickly tried to reel it in.

Vince jumped up and ran to the front, helping him as he struggled against the fight whatever he had caught was giving him.

My mom leaned back in her chair, seemingly bored with everything as Jane returned and brought me a bucket and a cold bottle of water from the ice chest.

I opened it and took a small sip, hoping that the water would be enough to quell the nausea.

My dad let out a celebratory shriek as he reeled faster, bringing a giant fish up the side of the boat before Vince reached out and grabbed it.

I took one look at it, and that was it. I turned around and threw up over the side of the boat.

"Abby!" My mom's voice drowned out the celebratory sounds coming from my dad and Vince at the front of the boat as she pulled everyone's attention to me. "What in the world are you doing?"

"She's not feeling well," Jane explained for me as I continued to hurl into the water.

"Sorry, pumpkin," my dad called from the front of the boat. "I didn't know you were so repulsed by bluefish. This one is a beauty though, probably well over twenty pounds."

I waved my hand behind me to get everyone to stop focusing on me and tried to give my dad a thumbs up.

"She gets so dramatic," my mother explained to Vince. "Always has to make everything about her and be the center of attention."

I didn't hear what he said to her, but a minute later, I felt his large, warm hand as it splayed across my lower back.

"Hey, are you okay?" he asked gently, not at all bothered by my current state.

"Yeah, thank you. I don't usually get motion sickness, but the choppy water got me today."

"Hey, sometimes it gets the best of us," he said with a smile as I turned around and sat down, taking the napkin that Jane handed me.

"With all of that, I would have thought she was pregnant," my mom snorted. "But we all know that'll never happen."

Jane and I exchanged a nervous glance as I wondered if my mom was right.

Seventeen
Abby

"How many packs did you buy?" Jane asked as she looked around the bathroom counter at the scattered pregnancy tests that I hadn't opened yet.

"Eight? Nine? I don't remember."

"You know each pack has two to three tests, right?"

"I wanted to be sure," I said with a groan.

"Okay, well, let's get started then."

I stared at the cup of urine sitting in the sink, wondering how I had gotten to this point in my life where I was hanging out with my sister on a Saturday night, dipping pregnancy tests in pee.

"I've never been so nervous," I admitted.

"Are you late?" she asked, opening the wrapper on one test while I unwrapped another. We dipped them at the same time and then put the caps back on.

"I don't know. I never figured out when I had my last period."

"Have you had one at all since we talked?"

"Nope," I replied, letting the p pop.

"And you guys fucked like rabbits for a full week, week and a half?"

"Yup."

"Have you and Vince—"

"No," I rushed out, thankful that at least I didn't have to stress about knowing who the father

 would be. Vince and I were getting along well, but it had only been a few weeks of dating, and I just hadn't felt that spark when he kissed me, so I never felt like letting it go further.

"Alright, we should know in two minutes."

She looked at her watch while I leaned against the wall and sank to the floor. I wasn't ready to know just yet, and I hated that this didn't feel how I thought it would. I imagined doing this with Nate, both of us excited as we waited to see whether we were starting a life together. Instead, I hadn't heard much from him since he went to Ocean City, other than that he would be home tomorrow, and I heard that from Capshaw when he answered Nate's phone while he was busy.

A few minutes passed by, which felt like hours. Jane looked at her watch, then down at me and smiled.

"It's time," she said softly.

I pushed myself up from the floor and took a deep breath. With a shaky hand, I reached for one of the tests but then immediately pulled back and shook my head.

"I can't do it. Can you just tell me?"

She nodded and picked up the first test, covering her mouth with her hand. Before saying anything, she picked up the other one and tears filled her eyes.

I knew at that moment what they said but still needed to hear her say it.

"You're going to be a mom!"

Eighteen
Nate

The sun had barely risen when I pulled into my driveway and found Abby waiting outside on the doorstep. I quickly put my truck in park and jumped out, rushing over to make sure she was okay.

"Abby, what are you doing here?" I asked, sitting down beside her.

She looked tired but fine overall. No bleeding wounds or sharp objects were protruding from her body.

"I talked to Capshaw, and he said that you guys would be back this morning."

Okay. I nodded, waiting for her to tell me what was going on. If that asshole Vince broke her heart in the few weeks I was gone, I was going to rip him to shreds.

"Abby, you're worrying me. What's wrong?"

"Can we go inside and talk?"

"Sure," I nodded, standing up and extending my hand to help her up.

Once we were inside, I went to the kitchen and started a pot of coffee. I was exhausted and had planned to come home and faceplant into my bed so I could crash for a few hours, but now that she was here, I wanted to make sure that I was awake and alert for whatever was going on.

"Okay, Abby—you're killing me. What's going on?"

She watched me nervously before digging into the pocket of her shorts and pulling something out. Her hand trembled slightly as she handed me two pregnancy tests.

"What's this?" I asked stupidly, knowing exactly what they were. One had two solid pink lines that meant she was pregnant, according to the key printed on the front. And if that wasn't clear, the digital one that read *pregnant* was as clear as day.

"I'm pregnant."

I licked my lips and took my time trying to figure out what to say. A million things rushed through my mind with a combination of excitement and happiness for her, but what actually came out was, "do you know whose it is?"

Her hand flew across my face in a heartbeat, taking me a second to register that she had slapped me.

"What the hell was that for?" I asked, stunned that she had done it. My hand flew up to my cheek, covering the spot that was still hot from her touch.

Tears filled her eyes, threatening to fall down her face as she tried to keep them in.

"How can you even ask me that? It's your baby, dumbass."

I blew out a breath and set the tests down on the counter.

"I'm sorry, Abby. I didn't mean to upset you. Things seemed to be going pretty well with Vince before I left, so you can't blame me for asking."

"I haven't slept with Vince, not that it's any of your business."

"How is it not my business, Abby?" I stepped toward her, lifting her chin with my finger as I forced her to look at me. "You're my best friend, first of all. Second, we were purposely trying to make a baby together. And third, Vince came into your life right at the same time that we were fucking non-stop. I'm not insinuating that you're easy, Abby, but who knows what happened in the few weeks that I was gone."

She pulled her chin from my grip and looked away.

"Even if I had slept with him, I wouldn't be pregnant within three weeks."

"I don't know how all of this works," I replied, throwing my hands in the air. "It feels like it's been a lot longer than that, and honestly, all I was thinking about was that babies come from having sex, and if you guys had sex then I should at least consider that I might not be the father."

She stopped for a moment, my words seeming to register something inside her.

"I'm sorry," she said quietly. "I shouldn't have slapped you."

"It's okay, I get it. I'm sorry that I keep upsetting you."

"I'm just a mess right now," she laughed. "Everything was going fine until I started throwing up on the boat and my mom made a bitchy comment about me being pregnant. Everything feels like it's turned upside down since then."

"Have you told her?"

"No, I just found out last night. Jane was with me when I took the tests. I didn't want anyone else to know until I told you."

"Not even Vince?" I asked, instantly regretting the bitterness that came out with the question.

She chewed her lip nervously and shook her head.

"Does he know that we were trying?" My voice was softer as my shoulders relaxed slightly. I wasn't trying to be a dick to her and hated that I felt so defensive about Vince. I knew I didn't have any right to be upset about her relationship with him, but that didn't help to calm the jealous beast that kept threatening to roar inside me and claim what I wanted to be mine.

"I thought about telling him, but it was never the right time."

"When are you going to tell him?"

"I haven't thought about that yet. I guess I wanted to talk to you first."

"Why me?" I folded my arms over my chest, hoping she would say something to ease the anxiety that continued to bubble up inside. Or maybe it was a subconscious movement to protect my heart that I feared she was on the verge of breaking.

"Because you're still my best friend, Nate. Or at least I hope that you are. And you're the baby's dad. That means that from here on out, we'll make decisions about stuff together."

"But how does Vince fit into that picture then? He's not going to want to sit on the sidelines while his girlfriend is off having a baby with her best friend."

"I don't know. I don't have the answers to your questions."

"Well, I think you need to sit down and talk to him. If things are serious between you, and you really like him, you owe it to him to tell him what's going on, Abby."

"I know," she sighed. "I'm just scared."

"Scared about what?"

"That he'll freak out and leave."

It felt like a knife pierced my heart and twisted around it, strangling the life out of me.

"Well, at least you'll still have me."

I noticed the emotion flash across her face before she pushed it away and pulled her shoulders back.

"I'm sure you're tired and want to get some rest so I'll let you go, I just wanted you to know before I tell anyone else. I'm going to try to get a doctor's appointment this week but you don't have to go with me."

"I'll be there," I said, pinning her with a look so she knew that I meant it.

"You don't have to."

"I know. I want to."

Nineteen
Abby

I wiped my mouth and then quickly rinsed my face under the cold water in the sink. When women said that morning sickness sucked—they weren't lying. I had barely found out I was pregnant less than a week ago, and it seemed like once I saw those two pink lines on the test, my body immediately morphed into a constant nausea factory.

The week had gone by painstakingly slow with Nate and I not talking to each other as much as we usually do. To top off an already lousy week, Vince found out that I was pregnant last night at dinner when I threw up after he served me a medium-rare steak that was more rare than medium. Once I cut into it and blood ran across the plate, I tossed my napkin on the table and darted for the bathroom.

When I returned to the table, a scowl was etched on his face, and he had the nerve to ask me about my *eating disorder*. I tried not to laugh in his face, but a woman like me doesn't get the curves that I have from *not* eating. When his concern didn't lift, I had to come clean about why I was constantly sick.

I had hoped that he would be more open-minded, but it turns out that when you're just starting to date someone and get to know them, they're not really on board with you being knocked up by your best friend. Bummer. He kindly let himself out of his own apartment to *get some air* while I grabbed my things and left the crime scene-looking dinner still untouched on the table. I stopped by the gas station on my way and talked myself out of reaching for the sushi when I remembered that I was pregnant. That and gas station sushi had a bad reputation as it was already.

This morning I tried to put enough makeup on to hide the dark circles under my puffy eyes but gave up. It was Friday, I had the day off, and my doctor's appointment was a quick ultrasound which meant no one was even going to be looking at my face. I finished getting ready and headed out the door, not bothering to text Nate to remind him. If he wanted to be there, he would.

I got checked in a few minutes early and sat down in the waiting room. The walls were painted a light yellow with framed pictures of newborn babies in different outfits. One had angel wings, one was wearing a cowboy hat, but my favorite was the one wearing a crocheted turtle shell.

I found myself grinning stupidly at it when the door opened, and Nate walked in. I swallowed hard, trying to force my eyes not to focus on the way his body looked more muscular under his t-shirt than usual. It wasn't unlike him to throw himself into working out when he was stressed, but given how filled out he looked, I started to wonder just how stressed he had been.

"Hey," he said, taking the seat next to me and pulling his leg to the side to make sure it didn't touch mine.

I felt the sting of it, knowing that whatever line we had initially crossed had been erased, and a new one was drawn, creating an even bigger divide in our friendship.

"Hi," I answered quietly, thankful when the nurse came out and called my name a few seconds later. We got up and followed her back to the exam room, listening to her directions before she left to give me privacy to get changed.

Nate turned away, looking out the window while I undressed from the waist down. I hopped onto the exam table and pulled the sheet over my lap, ensuring I wasn't showing any of my lady bits on accident.

A few minutes later, there was a knock on the door, and then a very attractive doctor I had never seen before walked in.

"Abby Hughes?" he asked, looking from the chart to me. His dark eyes looked between Nate and me while a brilliant smile crossed his face.

"That's me," I muttered, fidgeting my hands on my lap.

"I'm Doctor Nicoli. It's a pleasure to meet you."

He extended a hand to Nate, who took the initiative to introduce himself when my brain failed to produce any words. It wasn't because he was drop-dead gorgeous—he was—but I had been expecting Doctor Greenway, the woman who had been the town's gynecologist since I was born and looked nothing like the man in front of me.

"Sorry," I mumbled. "I was expecting to see Doctor Greenway today."

"Yes, I see. I apologize; she had a family emergency and asked if I could fill in for her today."

"Oh," I breathed, trying not to allow the weight of disappointment to overwhelm me. It wasn't that I was against having a male doctor, I had just been set on having Doctor Greenway, and this threw a little curve at me that I hadn't been expecting.

I shifted on the table, pulling the sheet lower over my legs while he sat on the stool and turned on the computer screen. A few minutes later, he had everything set up and turned to look at me.

"Shall we get started?"

I nodded and leaned back against the bed, unsure where to put my hands, so I kept them folded in my lap before deciding to hold onto the pillow behind my head. Why was I so nervous about this? Okay—that was a stupid question.

My breathing was getting heavier as the panic and anxiety started coursing through me. I watched as the doctor squirted some lube onto a wand that was covered with what looked like a condom. Nate reached down and grabbed my hand, squeezing it gently. I looked up at him, thankful that he was there. I should have known that he would be, but everything lately had me doubting a lot.

The doctor walked me through everything and asked me to relax as he slid the wand inside, navigating it easily. I was so focused on not hyperventilating from the nerves rushing through me that I almost missed it when something popped up on the computer screen.

He kept the wand still with one hand while using the other to turn some of the knobs on the computer. Seconds later, a loud swooshing sound echoed through the room with a faint thumping sound that sounded very much like a heartbeat.

"Is that the…."

I couldn't bring myself to say it, too afraid to get my hopes up.

He smiled and nodded.

"That's your baby's heartbeat."

<u>Twenty</u>
Nate

I wanted to run out of the doctor's office, waving the sonogram pictures in the air and shouting, "my baby has a heartbeat"! But I didn't. Not because I wasn't on top of the fucking world that I was having a baby, and so far, everything looked great, but because Abby had gone from ecstatic to crying on the exam table within seconds.

Between the doctor and me, we both tried to figure out what had her so upset as she cradled her head in her hands and sobbed. She shook her head, frustrated that she didn't know what was wrong, but she just couldn't stop crying. Doctor Nicoli squeezed her knee and gave her a reassuring smile as he promised her that all of this was completely normal. While he explained that her hormone levels were changing and that she might experience some intense mood swings, I had a feeling that I knew what the real source of the problem was.

Once we were done and she was dressed, we waited for the receptionist to schedule Abby's next appointment and then left. I walked with her to her car and kept my hands shoved into my pockets so I didn't reach out and touch her like I really wanted to do.

"Thanks for coming today," she said quietly, reaching for the car handle.

"I wouldn't miss it for the world, Abby. I told you that from the beginning, I'm all in."

"I know," she sighed with her head down so she didn't have to look me in the eye.

"Hey," I said, lifting her chin with my finger. "What did you have for breakfast?"

She pulled her brows together and thought about it.

"Ummm…"

"You didn't eat, did you?"

"I was going to, but then I got sick, and nothing sounded good."

I laughed and shook my head.

"Come on, let's get you fed."

"You don't have to feed me," she objected, tilting her head to the side.

"I was talking to the baby," I lied. "You can't stop me from taking care of it, and I heard it say that it wants bacon."

Her eyes lit up with delight and she subtly licked her lips.

"It did not."

"Did too. Specifically—it wants a BLT with some sea salt and vinegar kettle chips."

She sighed heavily and then looked up at me, her honey-colored eyes shimmering beneath her thick lashes.

"Damn you."

"What?" I shrugged a shoulder. "Can't blame me for knowing what you like. I'll meet you at my place?"

"Alright."

"Don't sound so enthused," I teased, pressing the button to unlock my truck. Once she was inside her car and had the ignition started, I jumped in my vehicle and led the way, feeling giddy with excitement that maybe our friendship could go back to the way it was before.

Abby sat on the couch and flipped through the channels on the TV while I cooked the bacon and got everything ready for the sandwiches. I didn't have to ask her how she wanted hers because I already knew that she wanted mayo on the side with the tomato because she loved how it tasted when the juice from the tomato mixed with the mayonnaise. That and she hated to have soggy bacon.

I finished and carried our plates to the living room, handing hers to her before sitting down and getting comfortable. There was still an odd tension between us, but overall it felt almost like old times. You know—before I fucked her nonstop for a week and a half and knocked her up.

She took a bite of her sandwich and moaned, covering her mouth with her hand while her eyes rolled back in her head.

"Oh my God, this is delicious."

I smiled pridefully, thankful that it didn't backfire on me and make her sick instead.

"I'm glad you like it."

"Seriously, Nate, thank you for this. I haven't been able to find anything to eat all week that hasn't made me sick. This is the first thing that the baby doesn't seem to mind letting me eat. I can tell already that this little one is going to be a picky eater," she joked.

My heart felt like it was swelling twice the size of what could fit inside my body. *My baby was a picky eater.*

"Well, just say when and I'll whip these up for you whenever you want them."

She tossed her head back and laughed.

"No way, I can't afford to gain that much weight. Can you imagine how high my cholesterol would be if I ate nothing but bacon every day?"

"Maybe the lettuce and tomato will offset it?" I joked with a crooked smile.

"I wish. Trust me, nothing has tasted this good in a while. You should come make these for me at the café, I bet we would have a line out the door every day."

"And give up my glamourous position of Captain?" I reached a hand up and pretended to flick something off my shoulder.

She rolled her eyes and took another bite, her attention back on the TV.

I did the same, ignoring the butterflies swarming in my stomach as I felt the heat from her body so close to mine.

When she was done, she leaned forward and set the empty plate on the coffee table next to mine. I could have gotten up to throw our trash away, but for once, I just wanted to sit and enjoy my time with her. In reality, I wanted to pick up her feet and move them to my lap while I rubbed them for her, but now that she was dating Vince, that would be really inappropriate.

As if reading my mind, she turned her attention to me and said, "Vince and I broke up."

My brows lowered, wondering if I had heard her correctly.

"Why? What happened?"

"He found out that I was pregnant and wasn't on board with it."

I tried to offer her a sympathetic smile, but it fell flat and never reached my lips.

"I'm sorry; I know you really liked him."

She gave a slight shrug and took a sip of water from the water bottle she had brought with her.

"Are you okay?"

"Yeah," she said on a heavy exhale. "It's not like we dated that long. I liked spending time with him, but I wasn't in love with him."

As much as I hated to admit it—I loved hearing her say that. At least I didn't have to worry about her harboring feelings for another man while carrying my baby. That was a selfish thing to think, but it wasn't like this whole *make a baby* thing was all my idea. She wanted it, and I wanted to help her. Now that we were having a baby, I wanted to believe that there was still a chance for us to be the happy family that I dreamed about.

"I'm still sorry."

She sat quietly for a few minutes before turning toward me and locking eyes.

"I'm the one who should be sorry, Nate."

"For what?"

"For a lot of things. We talked about doing this together, and then the second I meet someone, I run off and leave you to question everything that happened between us. I *hate* that I did that. I never wanted to be that girl—the one who walks away from their friends to be with some guy. You've been there for me since we were kids, and then I just bailed on you. I'm so sorry."

"Abby," I breathed, running a hand down the day-old stubble on my jaw. "I appreciate the apology, but I'm just as much to blame. As your best friend, I should have spoken up and told you that it bothered me that you were rushing into everything with Vince because it did—it bothered me so much to see you with him and to wonder whether he was touching you the way I had. But at the end of the day, Abby, the only thing that mattered to me was seeing you happy, and if that's what made you happy then who was I to stand in the way?"

A tear slid down her cheek as she quickly tried to wipe it away with the back of her hand.

"Ugh, hormones," she joked, crying harder.

I reached over and grabbed her hand, pulling her to me. Once she was on my side of the couch, I wrapped my arm around her and held her tightly against my chest as she laughed and cried and did all of the crazy things that hormones made you do.

Twenty-One

Abby

I woke up Saturday morning in Nate's bed to the smell of bacon and coffee floating down the hall. I groaned, then rolled out of bed, making a quick pitstop in the bathroom before heading to the kitchen where the goodness was coming from.

He was standing at the stove, shirtless with plaid pajama pants that hugged his ass just right, turning bacon in the pan. I tip-toed up behind him, peeking over his shoulder when he caught me. He reached behind and grabbed my hand, pulling it to his chest as he held it and kept cooking the bacon.

"Good morning," he said, and for a moment, I imagined a layer of sexiness that I wasn't sure was really there. Maybe I was hearing what I wanted to, or maybe these damn hormones were sneaking up on me again. For being so early in the pregnancy, I seemed to have an extra dose or two on board with the mood swings and increased sex drive. Call me crazy, but I didn't know many women who would willingly hump a pillow just to get some relief from the ache that was constantly spreading between their legs.

"Breakfast will be ready in a minute, but there's coffee if you want to make some."

"Oh, thank you," I said, pulling my hand back and standing flat on my feet again. "I don't think I'm supposed to have coffee because of the caffeine."

He turned his head and gave me the smile that could get me to do just about anything.

"I got a pack of decaf K-cups for you. There's a new bottle of creamer in the fridge too."

I pressed a hand to my heart, truly touched by the thoughtful gesture.

"Nate, you didn't have to do that."

His eyes roamed over my body, noticing the way his t-shirt pulled up on my thighs, almost revealing that I had nothing but panties on underneath. I quickly tugged it down but not before noticing a grin tug at his lips.

"It's not a big deal," he replied and turned back to the stove.

I popped a K-cup into the machine and inhaled as it started to brew. I had been a little disappointed that I would have to give up two things I loved the most—coffee and wine—but it was all worth it to have a baby. Now I was relieved that I could at least have coffee without feeling the weight of the guilt that I would put on myself for indulging in it.

I waited for it to finish brewing, added some creamer, and stirred it. Nate had finished cooking breakfast and was waiting for me to join him at the table. I sat down, careful not to spill the hot liquid, taking in the food in front of me.

Nate hadn't just cooked bacon—he had made an entire feast. There was bacon, sausage, hash browns, scrambled eggs—gag—pancakes, toast, and an assortment of jams and jellies set out between us.

"Wow, this is quite the spread," I commented as my mouth salivated and my stomach growled loudly.

He chuckled and arched a brow, letting me know he had heard it.

"My baby's hungry, gotta feed it."

I smiled, loving how much he was already taking to the baby and how happy he seemed about it. Much different than Vince, but then again, I couldn't blame him. I wouldn't stick around if I had just started dating someone and found out they were pregnant with their best friend's baby. No. Way.

I filled my plate with food and excitedly looked across it, trying to figure out what to eat first. Everything looked and smelled delicious, which was a nice change. I decided to start with the sausage and pierced one of the links with my fork before lifting it to my mouth and taking a bite.

It was the perfect combination of flavors that hit my tastebuds all at once, causing me to close my eyes and groan. I chewed slowly, savoring every single bit of it.

"Fuck, Abby," Nate groaned, tossing his fork on his plate.

My eyes popped open in alarm.

He gripped the side of the table as if he needed it to keep him in place. There was a hunger in his eyes that I had seen many times already and knew what it meant.

"Sorry," I whispered, setting my fork down on my plate as well.

In seconds, he was out of his seat and pushing mine back before he lifted me into his arms and carried me down the hall to his bedroom.

I squealed in delight, feeling his strong hand gripping my ass as he held me against his body.

"But my bacon," I cried, reaching my hand out for it.

He grunted and stopped for a moment, closing his eyes in frustration before turning around and returning to the table. He lowered enough for me to grab my plate from the table, then turned and marched us back to his room.

I giggled as I popped a piece of bacon in my mouth and smiled at him as I chewed it.

"You're lucky you're so fucking adorable and that my baby loves bacon so much," he grumbled, lowering me to my feet instead of tossing me on the bed.

"Why's that?" I asked, feeling cocky as I held a piece of bacon and pointed it at him.

"Because I'm about to fuck you senseless again, and there's not a woman in the world who I would usually let in my bed with a plate full of greasy food."

I pulled my lower lip between my teeth and felt that familiar ache between my thighs as I thought about him fucking me senseless.

"I'll be good, I promise."

His brow raised in doubt as he hooked his thumbs into the waistband of his pajamas and let them fall to the floor. I slowly chewed my bite, trying not to choke as I stared at the glorious beast that had gotten us into this situation to begin with.

Twenty-Two
Nate

"Well, that has to be a first," I said breathlessly as I wiped my mouth and crawled up to lay beside Abby on the bed. "I think you got bacon in my hair."

"Sorry," she laughed. "I was already committed to eating it when you decided to eat me, and I didn't realize how sensitive I was down there. I didn't expect it to happen so quickly."

"Yeah, I barely had time to take one last breath before you put me in a vice grip and locked your legs around my head."

"Sorry for that too," she giggled, a faint blush covering her face. "I really don't know what came over me. I've never been this horny before."

"I can tell. I'm pretty sure you demanded that I say your name before you slapped me with a sausage and forced my head back between your thighs. I mean, I'm not complaining, I just don't think I've ever eaten a girl out that literally tasted like breakfast."

"I told you not to make me touch myself, my hands were still covered in grease."

"That's why you had a fork."

"There was no time to worry about that!" She tossed her head back and laughed. "I had the best of *all of the worlds*!

I was eating bacon and sausage while you were eating me. What more could I ask for?"

"True," I teased, laying a hand flat against her now naked stomach. "I still can't believe there's a baby in there."

She placed her hand on top of mine, and we stared at them linked together.

"I know, me neither."

"Hearing the heartbeat yesterday was so amazing. I can't wait to tell my mom."

"Do you think she'll be happy about it?" Abby asked, tilting her head to look up at me.

"Absolutely. She's been waiting for me to knock you up for years."

"Nate!" She reached over and swatted my arm playfully.

"No, but seriously I think she's going to be ecstatic that she's going to be a grandma and that we're doing this together. She just adores you, Abby. Always has."

She took a deep breath and looked away. I could tell something was bothering her.

"What's wrong?" I asked, sliding my finger under her chin to turn her face back to me.

"Nothing."

"Abby."

"Ugh," she groaned with an eye roll. "How do you always know?"

"Because I know everything there is to know about you. Now spill it. What's wrong?"

She let her shoulders fall and then turned on her side to look at me.

"I'm worried about how my parents will take it."

"You don't think they'll be happy?"

"I don't know. My mom got so obsessed with trying to marry Vince and me that I don't know if she's still even obsessed with grandbabies anymore. Maybe she never was? Maybe she just liked trying to control different pieces of my life because she's bored."

"What about your dad? How do you think he'll feel about it?"

She squinted her eyes and winced.

"I'm pretty sure he will want to kill you."

"Great, I'm looking forward to telling them tonight," I grumbled, covering my face with my hand.

I loved spending the day with Abby, cuddling together as if nothing had happened. It was weird how easily we fell into this pattern with each other, not bothering to stop and question anything. I knew that we needed to sit down and talk about what this thing was between us, but for now, I was just happy that I had my Abby back.

Twenty-Three
Abby

"Ugh, why doesn't anything fit me anymore?" I groaned as I rolled onto the bed and tried to pull a pair of leggings over my round stomach. "We don't need a turkey when I'm officially as big as one."

"You look beautiful," Nate said, holding his hand out to help me off the bed. "And if you were a turkey, you'd be the most delicious one I've ever eaten."

"Stop it," I laughed, pushing his hands away as they tried to roam over my breasts while he held me from behind. "We're going to be late to dinner at my mom's."

"So, what's a few minutes?"

"It's Thanksgiving, and she's cooking—two of her least favorite things."

"We could stay here," he offered, nipping at my ear as he kissed down the side of my neck.

"Soon, you're going to have to stop being afraid of my dad."

"It's been five months, and he still won't look me in the eye. It's like he knows all of the crazed, perverted stuff I've done to you."

"He'll get over it once the baby is here. You'll see."

I turned and hugged him, resting my head on his chest as he rubbed my back.

It was true, my dad had been angry with Nate ever since he found out that he got me pregnant. While my mom was upset about Vince and me breaking up, she was over it quickly when we showed her the sonogram picture of her grandbaby. She's been over the moon and trying to buy baby stuff for us ever since. My dad, on the other hand, had yet to come around, and part of me felt like maybe it was because things with Nate and I never shifted into something more than just two best friends who were having a baby together. It wasn't that I needed Nate to propose to me and promise me the white picket fence, but it was also the topic of gossip around town that he wasn't willing to settle down and be with the woman he was having a child with.

"How long do we have to stay?" he asked while helping me put my coat on. I was purposely trying to hold off on buying maternity clothes until I had to, which meant that I was struggling to get most of my clothes on because they were all threatening to burst at the seams.

"Dinner and dessert. Then we can go."

"What if I want to come home and have dessert here?"

"I like the dirty thoughts in your head, but I'm not leaving until I get my cherry pie with extra whipped cream."

Nate tickled my sides, making me squeal, before helping me out to the car.

Dinner was ready when we got there, which was surprising but helped ease some of the awkward tension between my dad and Nate. I sat down between them and made an effort to ask Jane about work and then talked with Sally and Mikey about school to fill the rest of the silence. The last thing I wanted today was to draw attention to myself.

I kept talking when Nate gently rubbed a hand along my thigh under the table, pulling my attention to him. He nodded at my food, and I realized that my plate was still untouched while everyone else was almost done with dinner.

I listened as Sally told me the silly joke she had learned at school and started eating my dinner. I was trying to pay attention to what she was saying, but the moment I tasted the food, I closed my eyes and moaned. Everything tasted amazing, and suddenly, I felt ravenous.

When I opened them, I found everyone silently staring at me around the table. I swallowed hard and tucked my chin to my chest as I kept eating.

"Well, at least Abby still has her appetite," my mom commented before taking a sip of her wine. "When I was pregnant, my morning sickness was so bad that I couldn't hold anything down. I ended up *losing* weight, which helped me bounce right back after I had her."

I looked away, starting to push my plate to the side even though I hadn't finished my food. Nate subtly held his hand out and stopped me. I caught his eye, and he gave me a soft smile as he pushed it back to me.

I knew what he was saying without having to hear him say the words. It was the same things he had been telling me for the past five months, ever since we announced my pregnancy and my mom tossed in comments about my weight and how hard it would be to get my body back at my age. We didn't have to talk about it, he always just knew how I was feeling and made an effort to show my body special attention when I started feeling down about myself.

Once dinner was over, my dad retired to the living room while Nate convinced my mom to show him her new seashell collection, and Jane and I cleaned up. It was a given that we would do the dishes, but it was a thousand times more peaceful not to have my mom in there, hovering over us.

"So, how are you feeling?" Jane asked as she filled the sink with hot water.

I piled the plates on the counter beside her and finished clearing the table.

"I started to get some energy back, but it disappeared as quickly as it came. Now I just feel like a lump of coal, ready to explode in everything I wear."

"Have you bought any maternity clothes yet?"

"Not yet, I was trying to hold off to see how long I could wear what I already have." I looked down at the dress that stretched so tightly over my chest and stomach that the fabric was almost see-through. "But I think those days are over."

"We can go shopping this weekend if you want. The kids will be with Rick, so I'm going to start some Christmas shopping."

"Okay, that would be great. I work tomorrow, but I'm off on Saturday."

"Perfect; I'll pick you up around eight?"

I snapped the lid on the Tupperware and turned to look at her.

"Fine," she laughed. "Nine?"

"You're lucky that I love you," I teased. "I'll be ready."

"Ready for what?" my mom asked as she breezed into the kitchen.

I felt my body tense at the sound of her voice.

"Jane's taking me shopping."

"For what?"

"Clothes."

"Oh, I see. I never had that *issue*."

I rolled my eyes and tossed the container into the fridge with the rest of the food. I stood there for a few minutes, letting the cold air tickle my skin and cool me off. When I closed the door, she stood on the other side, watching me.

"Not all of us are as lucky as you were, mom," I muttered and walked past her.

"Well, it's nothing to be upset about. Have you talked to Doctor Greenway about how much weight you should be gaining?"

I sat down at the table and blew a breath out, not in the mood to have this conversation with her. I could help Jane finish up the dishes, but there was hardly any room over there, to begin with, and my big pregnant stomach made it an even tighter space.

"I'm not seeing Doctor Greenway, mother. I've told you that."

"Well then, maybe you could have your sister take over your care."

"What am I going to do?" Jane blurted out, spinning around with a thick layer of bubbles on her hand.

"You know about babies," my mom said evenly.

"I'm a pediatrician, mom. Not an OBGYN."

She waved a hand dismissively as if it didn't matter.

"It's not that different. Both of them deal with babies and kids."

Jane shook her head and went back to washing the dishes, ignoring our mother. It was no secret that our mother had never taken much of an interest in Jane's life either and knew very little about what she did as a pediatrician.

"I just don't like you seeing that *other* doctor," my mom muttered as Nate walked in.

"What's wrong with Doctor Nicoli?" he asked, sitting beside me. "He's been wonderful with Abby. We both like him a lot."

My mom scoffed and scowled at him.

"I just don't think a man has any business down there."

Butterflies swarmed my stomach as I thought about all of the *business* Nate had done down there and was likely to do as soon as we got back to my place. We had yet to move in with each other—you know, since we were still just friends that were having a baby together.

"It's perfectly fine, mom. He's a doctor, not a creep with a video camera and a webpage."

"Well, it seems he could have been another kind of doctor, but yet he *chose* to do this. I just think that he has ulterior motives, and you should be more selective with who you let down there. It's not a free ride at the fair, Abby."

"Oh my God, mom!" I slammed my hand down on the

table, startling everyone in the room, including my dad, who had just walked in. "Doctor Nicoli doesn't care about my vagina and isn't checking it out. He NEVER even sees it, and the few times that he has, both Nate and a female nurse have been in the room. I hate to break it to you, but he's not a pervert, and he's been an amazing doctor that has made me feel nothing but comfortable. I'm not going to stop seeing him just because your head is on crooked."

"Abby—" my mom started before my dad cut her off.

"Enough, Rhonda. Abby is a grown woman, and if she's comfortable with her doctor, then that's all there is to it. I won't have you attacking her on her decisions anymore."

My jaw hit the floor as I watched my dad cross the room, grab a bottle of water from the fridge, clap a hand on Nate's shoulder, then head back to the living room where he had come from. My mother lifted her chin and gave me an icy cold glare before getting up and leaving the room, letting the door swing behind her.

"What the hell just happened?" Jane asked quietly, looking between Nate and me.

"I have no freaking idea."

"I thought your dad still hated me," Nate mumbled, rubbing his hand over the spot where my dad had shown him affection.

"Well, I can't imagine that things are going to stay as calm as they are now, so I'm going to get the kids ready and head out. Did you want me to cut you guys a slice of pie?"

"I can go do it," Nate offered, gently rubbing my back before going to the dining room where the pies were still on display.

"I've never seen dad talk to mom like that," I said in disbelief.

Jane finished the last few dishes and put them away before turning to face me.

"I was here the other day, and they were fighting a lot. I don't know what's going on, but something is definitely different with them."

I tried to smile but gave up when it took too much energy.

Nate came in a few minutes later with two paper plates filled with pie. I grabbed the foil from the counter and covered them.

"Jane, do you need help with anything before we go?" I asked, sliding into my coat Nate had brought me.

"I'm good, but thanks."

We hugged, and she went off to fix plates of pie for her and the kids while I went in search of my parents. My mom was upstairs in her room with the door locked, so I didn't bother. Instead, I went to the living room and sat on the armrest of my dad's recliner and waited for his show to go to commercial so I could say goodbye.

When a woman appeared on the TV, talking about diaper cream, he kept his eyes focused on her but lifted his hand to my knee and gently patted it.

"You know, your mom hasn't always been this way."

"What do you mean?"

"She used to be happy. So was I."

My heart clenched, and I reached down and squeezed his hand. My father was one of my favorite people—even if he hadn't been on board with Nate and I having a baby until now—and to hear that he wasn't happy created a deep sadness inside of me.

"I'm sorry, dad. I didn't know that you weren't happy."

"It's not your job to know, honey. As your parents, we should only be focused on your happiness. You shouldn't have to worry about ours. I'm the one who should be sorry," he laughed softly. "I was so thrown off with you and Nate having a baby that I didn't stop and realize that it made *you* happy. That's all I've ever wanted for you and your sister, Abby. For my grandbabies. Nate is a wonderful man, and I know he'll be the best father to that baby, just like he's always been your best friend."

I wiped a tear from my eye and tried to blink the rest away.

"But daddy, I hate that you're not happy. How long have you felt that way?"

He puffed his cheeks full of air, then let it out as he thought about it, rubbing his other hand across his brow.

"You know, I don't know. But I finally realized it when we were out on the boat for the Fourth of July. I was so excited and proud to pull in that fish, and you know what your mother said to me?"

"What?"

"Not a damn thing. She couldn't have cared less. All she cared about was making Vince like her because she needed that attention from him. But I couldn't blame her because I wanted his attention to. I wanted that buddy to help pull in that damn beast and then celebrate with me afterward like he did."

"Dad," I whispered. "I'm so sorry that you've felt so alone."

"It was a wake-up call after that. I saw you go after what you wanted with Nate, and Abby, I've never been prouder in my life. You didn't sit around and wait for something to happen, *you made it happen*. That's when I realized that I was just sitting here, living the life that was being given to me because *I* wasn't willing to go make something happen."

"What do you want to happen?"

He turned in his recliner and looked up at me, his brown eyes soft as the wrinkles crinkled with his smile.

"I just want to be happy. I want to do things that make me feel fulfilled. I want to go on trips and live a life of adventure. I don't want to just sit here and allow life to pass by me."

Before I could say anything, my mom came down the stairs and entered the living room, standing before my father and me with her hands folded in front of her.

"I'm sorry for earlier, Abby. I was out of line, and I can see that now."

They exchanged a look that I hadn't seen between them before. *What was that? Warmth? Compassion? Understanding?* Love.

"It's okay," I muttered, unsure what else to say. I couldn't remember the last time my mother had ever apologized to me—and come to think of it, I don't think she ever had.

"Your mother and I were planning to tell you guys after dinner, but that didn't happen," my dad said, getting up from his chair as I slowly stood so I didn't get knocked over. "Jane, Nate, can you come in here for a minute?"

I held my breath, wondering if they were going to tell us they were getting divorced. Everything was so surreal and different tonight that it wouldn't surprise me any.

The door swung open, and Jane came in with Sally and Mike in front of her and Nate behind her. We all filled the small space of the living room as my parents stood in front of us, arms wrapped behind each other's backs as they hugged. My dad planted a kiss on her temple and then cleared his throat.

"I know we always do things as a family and spend the holidays together, but this year, your mother and I won't be here for Christmas."

My eyes almost popped out of my head as I studied them and how my mom looked up adoringly at my father.

"We're leaving on Sunday and going on a three-month vacation in Europe. We'll be back at the end of February and hopefully before the baby comes."

I didn't know what to say as I stood there watching them with a hand covering my mouth. Nate slid behind me and wrapped a hand around my waist, somehow knowing I needed that hug more than I realized.

"You guys are going to be gone for three months?" I stammered.

They both nodded, a sudden look of sympathy on my mother's face as she saw my reaction. It felt like I was in a parallel universe with someone who looked like my mother but yet was not acting like her.

"But I'm due on March fourteenth. What if the baby comes early?"

"You'll be fine, dear," she said with a smile. "Nate will be here, and Jane. You'll have plenty of help and support until we can get back. And I promise—if you go into labor while we're gone, we will be on the first plane back."

"Not that I'm not happy for you guys," Jane said, speaking up from the back of the room. "But why now? This is all so sudden."

"It was either this or a divorce," my dad replied before sharing another look with my mom. "We knew that if we wanted to save our marriage, we needed to get away and find ourselves again. Find what makes us happy and rekindle that spark that used to be so hard to put out."

"Divorce?" Jane squealed, her eyes pushing the limits around her sockets as they bulged.

"It's no secret that we've been unhappy for quite some time. I've worked my ass off my entire life and built up decent savings that I'll never be able to use before I die if I just sit around Beaumont Creek. It's about time we go see the world and live life." My dad let out a heavy sigh and squeezed my mom tighter.

"We promise to bring back some wine if that makes it better?" she said and looked between Jane and me as if she knew the way to our hearts. Okay—she did.

We said goodbye, and I found myself hugging my parents a little tighter than normal while I processed this sudden news. Not only had my parents been on the brink of divorce, but now they were leaving on a three-month romantic vacation through Europe, all right before I had the baby. I tried to remind myself that I still had Nate and Jane and that I wouldn't be without the support that I needed. I was a strong, independent woman who could do this without needing anyone else.

Twenty-Four
Abby

Right at nine o'clock, Jane's horn honked in my driveway, letting me know she was there. I groaned and grabbed my keys and phone from the counter, and locked the door. She was bouncing to the music in her car, clearly a morning person, while I scowled and looked like someone ran over my puppy.

I was used to getting up early for work, but ever since I started the second trimester of my pregnancy, mornings were even harder. Sherry and I had even switched some of our shifts so she could open and I could close since it was easier for me at this point.

"Good morning!" she sang as I opened the door and plopped into the passenger seat. I gave her a snarky smile and buckled my seatbelt, pulling it across the too-tight shirt that wrapped around my swollen stomach.

Jane smiled and reached over to give the bump a quick rub before pulling out of the driveway and heading to the store. We had a list of places we were going to in Cape May, but my stomach chose that moment to alert her to the fact that I hadn't eaten breakfast yet.

She glanced at me with a wary look before pulling off the freeway and taking the first exit to a fast-food restaurant. It was no surprise to anyone that I got hangry before I was pregnant, but now that there were two of us in the same body—it was like worrying about a nuclear detonation if we weren't fed in a timely manner.

Five minutes later, I was chowing down on an egg and bacon biscuit sandwich while Jane got back on the road and sang along to the radio as she drove. I devoured the food in minutes, then washed it down with the orange juice she ordered for me.

"Thank you," I said, blotting my mouth with a napkin before tossing it into the paper bag with the rest of my trash.

She smiled and gave me a quick wink before returning her focus to the road.

"So, do you have a list of what you're looking for today?" I asked, knowing that she planned to finish all her Christmas shopping while she had a free day without the kids. She would spend the whole day shopping, then go home, wrap their presents, and hide them before their dad dropped them off tomorrow morning. It was a lot of work, but she never seemed to mind.

"I have a general list, but nothing too specific, which makes it harder this year."

She drummed her fingers on the steering wheel, but I could see the tension in her shoulders.

"What's Rick getting them?" I asked, going directly to what I assumed was the source of her stress. She always tried to get them smaller, more meaningful gifts, while he tried to outdo her and get the biggest, most expensive ones he could find.

"One of those obnoxiously big cars that they can drive themselves. You know, the ones that cost like five hundred dollars, and no one has room for them."

"Why don't you just tell him it has to stay at his place?"

"Because he just bought that new condo, and there is literally no room for them to play in the sparse grass, let alone ride that thing."

"Then tell him to get them something else. You don't owe him anything, and it's quite presumptuous that he thinks he can give them that, and then you have to deal with it afterward."

"Have you met Rick?" she laughed, slowing down and turning her turn signal on as she waited for the light. "He's the definition of presumptuous."

I reached over and squeezed her arm to get her attention. When she turned to me, I said, "if mom and dad can take a three-month vacation together to save their marriage, you can stand up to your ex-husband."

Her shoulders slumped as she let out a heavy breath.

"You're right."

"I know I am," I said lightly as I pushed a handful of buttons on her dashboard.

"What are you doing?"

"Calling Rick."

"What?! Why?"

"Because if you don't tell him now, you're going to chicken out later, and then you'll end up with this beast of a toy car at your house on Christmas morning with kids who are so over the top excited about it that they don't care about any of their other gifts, and then you'll have to fight with them all day to get out of the car and go inside, and that's how the demise of your life will start," I said in one single, long-winded breath. "So, we're going to call him now, and you're going to tell him that the stupid car will not go to your house, nor will it be kept there."

She turned to the side and looked quizzically at me as the phone rang on the speakers throughout her car. A few seconds later, his deep voice answered the phone.

"What."

I flinched at his words, anger radiating through me at how he was speaking to my sister.

"I need to talk to you about the gift for the kids," Jane said sternly as she found a parking spot and pulled in. She put the car in park but left it running so the call didn't disconnect.

"What about it?"

She gripped the steering wheel hard, her knuckles turning white with anger.

"I don't want it at my house, so if you're going to get it for them, then you need to find a place to keep it at yours."

"You know there's no room at the Condo, Jane."

"Then maybe you should find something else for them for Christmas."

"Is this because you don't have enough money to buy them gifts this year? I'm not going to go cheap just because you can't—"

"Listen here, dickwad," I bit out angrily. "It's not about the money, it's about her saying no to having it at her house.

Either find a place to store it at your place, or don't buy it at all. But if you ever talk to my sister like that again, I will cut your dick off, hang it on a keychain, then parade it around town, showing everyone the world's tiniest dick."

Jane's eyes widened as she turned in her seat to look at me.

"I'm not having this conversation with you right now," he snarled into the phone.

"No—you're not having this conversation, period. If you buy the damn car, you'll have to explain to the kids why they can't keep it and why you have to take it back if you can't find room at your stupid condo. Talk to my sister this way again, and you're going to have even bigger issues to deal with," I warned.

The line clicked and went dead.

"Well, that went about as well as I had planned," Jane laughed, turning off the car and grabbing her purse from the backseat.

"Sorry," I said, suddenly feeling terrible for all of it. "I didn't mean to cause problems for you."

"Nah, it's alright. You were right, if I didn't talk to him about it now, I would have chickened out later and never would have said anything."

"Does he always treat you like that?" I asked once I was out of the car and we were walking to the store.

She shrugged like it was no big deal.

"He's such an ass."

"That's why I divorced him. But enough about that, let's go shopping!"

She looped her arm through mine and led me into the store, straight toward the maternity clothes section.

Two hours later, I had three hundred dollars worth of clothes in my shopping cart, but Jane kept reminding me that everything was on sale and that it was really only around a hundred dollars. I hated the idea of spending a lot of money on stuff I would only wear for a few months, but she assured me that they would come in handy after I had the baby and wanted something comfy to wear.

It felt weird to still call it *the baby,* but Nate and I had agreed that we didn't want to know the gender until birth. It definitely made it harder to try to decorate the nursery, but I didn't need to worry about that right now.

We went through the toy aisles as Jane scanned the options, looking for stuff for Sally and Mikey. As a doctor, she made plenty to buy expensive gifts for them, but she preferred to focus on the things that mattered, and growing up, we never cared about how much anything cost. It was always the little things or the handmade things that meant the most to us.

I browsed alongside her, checking to see what she was getting them so I could figure out what my gifts to them would be. Sally was six, and Mikey was eight, so it was getting harder to shop for them without buying Barbies and Legos that they possibly had outgrown already.

Jane picked up a few things from the shelf and tossed them into her cart, then scanned the contents.

"What am I missing?" she asked, more to herself than me. "I have new pajamas and a book for them to open on Christmas Eve. They both have four new outfits and a pair of shoes. I got the stuff to make gingerbread houses, candy canes for the tree, and hot chocolate mix." She moved things around in the cart and separated them into two separate piles, one for each child.

"I have two science experiment kits for Mikey, all of the baking stuff for Sally, and the little toys for their stockings. I feel like I'm missing…."

Her voice trailed off as she looked up at the shelf, and a smile spread across her face. She dropped the stuff in her hands and walked over to pick up the box.

"What's that?" I asked, standing beside her.

"It's this laser tag set that Mikey's been talking about. I totally forgot that he wanted it until now."

"That's great," I said enthusiastically but noticed the look on her face as she turned around and looked at the items in her shopping cart. "What's wrong?"

"If I get this, then I need to put something else back, and I can't decide what he'll want more."

"Well, why don't I get the science stuff for him, and you get the laser tag?"

"This is more expensive, so he'll have fewer gifts to open than Sally."

"Is there anything special she's been wanting that's more expensive?"

Jane tilted her head back and closed her eyes, trying to think.

I didn't rush her through it, knowing that something would come to her. A few minutes later, her eyes popped open, and she smiled excitedly.

"There's this doll house she's been talking about that one of her friends has. I think that's why she always wants to go over to their house—that and her mom lets them eat an endless amount of candy while she's there. I think it's about the same price, but I don't remember."

"Well, let's go look."

She led the way while I worked on moving the science kits and baking stuff from her cart to mine. That made my shopping a hell of a lot easier, and I was glad she was able to find something special for each of the kids that she really wanted to get. When she wasn't looking, I added a handful of candy bars to the cart and followed her to the aisle with the doll house. I might be their only aunt, but that didn't mean I wasn't going to spoil them to make me their favorite.

Twenty-Five
Nate

"Have you guys decided what color to paint the nursery?" my mom asked as I balanced the phone between my ear and shoulder.

"Not yet. We're going to get through Christmas, then we'll figure out all of that stuff."

"Is she having a baby shower?"

"I'm sure Jane is throwing her one, but I don't know the details."

"Why not?"

"Why would I?" I asked with more annoyance than I should have had with my mom.

"I just figured you would know more about what was happening since you're the baby's father."

And there it was. The touchy subject that I tried desperately to avoid every time we spoke, but she insisted on bringing up.

Abby had talked about the baby shower a handful of times, but I had no idea what they had decided on. She wanted to wait until her parents were back from Europe, but Jane thought it would be better to do it sooner in case the baby came early. That way, everything was set up, and she wasn't struggling to get clothes washed and furniture built with a newborn. Granted, I would be there to help, but it was still undecided what my ultimate role would be since we didn't live together, and Abby was turning her spare room into a nursery but hadn't asked me if I wanted to turn mine into one too.

"I'm not going to get into this with you again," I muttered.

"Fine," she said with a sigh. "Will I see you guys next week for Christmas?"

"Yeah, we'll be over in the day on Christmas Eve."

"You're not coming on Christmas day?"

"I actually had something special planned for Abby since her parents will be out of town, and this is the first time she's celebrated it without them."

"What about Jane and the kids?"

"We're going to do dinner on Christmas Eve with them and exchange gifts that night."

"Okay, I'll let your father know it'll be just us this year for Christmas."

"Are you upset that I won't be there?"

I lifted a stack of boxes and moved them from my desk to the floor as I continued to unpack the supplies that had come in this morning.

"No, not at all, honey. You'll be starting your own family soon, and I expect you'll have your own traditions that you'll want to do with your baby."

"Thanks, mom."

"I'll talk to you later. Be safe, I love you."

"Love you too."

I grabbed my phone and pressed the end call button before setting it on my desk. I hadn't talked to Abby about Christmas yet, but I knew that she had seemed down the past few days every time she talked about how her parents weren't going to be there. They had facetimed several times, and even I was surprised by how happy her father and mother both looked as they sipped on wine and showed us around wherever they were that day. Abby would have me hold the phone while she showed them her growing belly and how much it had changed since they saw her a month ago at Thanksgiving.

It was hard to believe that she was already six months pregnant and that in just a few months, we were going to have a baby. I had been focused on making Christmas extra special for her, including the gift that I had specially made in Ocean City that I needed to go pick up tomorrow when I was off shift.

I was packing stuff up and marking off the inventory list of the items received before I tracked down the other boxes that hadn't made it to my office when I heard a commotion outside my door. I put the clipboard down and walked down the hall into the common area to see the guys huddled in the middle around someone that they were clearly excited to see.

Hearing me approach, they parted, and standing there before me was Colin fucking Mitchell—Abby's high school sweetheart who was about to propose before he left with a football scholarship.

Twenty-Six
Abby

"How many more orders do we have left?" I asked Sherry as I sat down at the table and yawned.

"Only a few," she laughed, wiping down the counter after the morning rush.

It was exactly one week until Christmas, and this was one of our busiest times of the year when everyone came in to place orders for pies, cookies, and our *sex cake* that everyone was still talking about. I wasn't sure if it was the cake itself that was super popular or the fact that someone had leaked the name *sex cake,* and everyone was giggling about it like middle school girls.

I was feeling exhausted and knew that it was only going to get worse. I wasn't lucky like some women who got an energy boost in the second trimester. I was constantly tired and finding it harder and harder to get going each morning.

Sherry had opened this morning, which meant that I had a long day ahead of me since I was closing. I knew Nate was on shift as well, so I expected to see him and the guys in here at some point to get their sugar fix. Things there were super slow, and if I remembered correctly, they were supposed to be helping with the kids at the community center as they decorated for the annual holiday festival.

I had gone with Nate and helped out several times over the years, but I was too tired and too pregnant to be of any help this year. They would be responsible for hanging lights and setting up the booths for the local vendors, and the kids would handle the other decorations, including the hand-painted ornaments that would be placed on the giving tree by Santa's sleigh.

The door opened, and the rooster crowed while I pushed myself off of the chair to go help whoever had walked in. I rounded the corner and came face to face with someone—or more so, face to chest.

"Sorry," I said, stepping back and looking up.

My heart skipped a beat, and my stomach felt like it had dropped to the floor.

"Colin?" I breathed out his name, tilting my head to the side as if I didn't believe my eyes. "What are you doing here?"

"Hey, Abs. Good to see you. I came for some reinforcements," he laughed, stepping back to look in the display case. "I'm heading to my mom's, and you know how she is if I don't come bearing fresh pastries."

I swallowed past the lump in my throat and walked behind the counter. He looked through the cases, brushing his finger across his jaw as he decided.

"Can I get a dozen banana nut muffins, a dozen glazed donuts, and one chocolate éclair?"

He looked up at me, offering a dazzling smile that made his blue eyes shine. I stared at him longer than I should have, trying to remember the boy who left almost twenty years ago to play college football. The man in front of me looked similar, but now there were wrinkles by the corners of his eyes from years of smiling and muscles that hid well enough beneath his clothes to let you know that they were there without being over the top on display.

"You okay, Abby?" he asked after I failed to respond to him.

I shook my head, clearing the fog, and reached for a to-go box.

"Yeah, sorry," I laughed nervously, then began packing up the requested items. "So, you're headed to your parents?"

He nodded and shoved his hands into the pockets of his trousers, rocking back on his heels.

"It was time that I came back and spent Christmas with them."

I pulled my lips into a thin smile and focused on his order. Once the muffins were ready, I sealed the box, slid it down the counter to the register, and then worked on getting the donuts boxed up.

"How's your dad doing?" I asked, knowing his cancer had returned and he hadn't been doing well.

"He's tired. I think he's ready to go but doesn't want to leave my mom on her own."

"I'm so sorry," I whispered.

"Thank you. It will be hard on all of us when he passes, but I know it'll be devastating for my mom. That's why I decided to come back."

"You're back? Like for good?" I asked, dropping the tongs in my hand to the floor.

I didn't bother to pick them up, I just stood there staring at him, waiting for him to give me the answer I had wanted to hear for twenty-two years.

"Yeah, Abby. I'm back."

Twenty-Seven
Nate

"You know that's not how you hang lights," I scolded and pointed to the spot where they were hanging lower than the rest. "Get the ladder and have Capshaw help you fix it."

Jones nodded and took off to get the ladder. I walked around and checked out the rest of the lights, making sure they were correctly hung. How would it look if the *fire department* was responsible for creating a safety hazard?

Everything else looked great, and the place was really coming together. It was already Thursday afternoon, and I was dragging today. I regretted not making it to Rockin' Rooster before we got to the community center this morning, but we didn't have time thanks to Jones almost catching the kitchen on fire.

My head was pounding, so I went in search of a vending machine when I rounded the corner and ran into Jane.

"Hey," I said, pulling out my wallet while I waited for her to make her selection. "What are you doing here?"

"I came by to help the kids with the decorations. Mike and Sally are outside painting ornaments for the giving tree." She bent down, grabbed the diet soda bottle, and stepped to the side. "Are you guys here helping out too?"

I nodded and stuck my dollar into the machine, then entered

the code for a bottle of water.

"Yeah, they just finished getting the lights up. I need to find Caroline and see if she's ready for us to help with taping off the spots for the vendor booths."

"Sounds fun," she laughed, taking a drink and then putting the cap back on.

"I think I'd rather trade and help the kids paint," I joked. "At least I can trust them not to catch anything on fire."

Capshaw came around the corner, and his eyes lit up when he saw Jane.

"Hey, Doc, how's it going."

"Capshaw."

"Are you ever going to give me the opportunity to thaw that heart of yours so you'll give me a chance?"

Her brows rose then her eyes narrowed.

"It's not my heart that's frozen, Capshaw. It's that I'm too smart to trust that a man like you wants something more than just sex. And honestly, I'm just not interested in a casual relationship, nor do I want someone I have to babysit. I got divorced for a reason. Trust me when I say that I'm good."

I covered my mouth with my hand to hide the laughter that bubbled up from behind it.

"See you next week," she said with a warm smile before turning and walking away.

Once she was gone, he turned to me with a look of complete defeat on his face.

"Why is she always so mean to me?"

"Because you come at her like a horny fifteen-year-old, and she's forty-one. She's over the games and cheesy pick-up lines. Maybe act like yourself, and she'll come around."

"Do you really think I have a chance?" he asked with hope in his voice.

"Nope," I said, letting the p pop. I clapped a hand on his shoulder and went back to check on the rest of the guys.

By five o'clock, everything was done and ready for the holiday festival to start tomorrow. It was a three-day event, beginning on Friday and ending Sunday evening, allowing everyone in Beaumont Creek to have a chance to stop by and check out the vendor booths and finish up their last-minute shopping. Santa would be here the entire time for the kids to take pictures with and leave their wish lists with his elves, and people would stop by the giving tree to purchase the ornaments the kids had painted. All of the money from the ornaments went to the families in town who needed a little extra help during the holidays, and people had the option to drop off wrapped gifts under the tree as well. It was truly a magical, wonderful time of year in Beaumont Creek, and I looked forward to it each year.

I grabbed my phone out of my pocket, took a picture of the table already set up for Rockin' Rooster, and sent it to Abby. They had hired a few temporary employees to help with the holiday rush, which was great since Abby needed to be off of her feet more often these days. Sherry would manage things at the café, while Abby and Bobbie handled things at the festival. With enough hands on deck, things should go smoothly, but that didn't mean I didn't purposely find the largest space available for her booth. I even snuck in a few extra chairs for her to be able to put her feet up when needed.

I waited for her to respond to my message, but nothing came. It was time to head out, so I gathered the guys, and we headed back to the station to finish our shift. While it should have been an easygoing night where I could sleep unless we got called out, I felt restless and couldn't shake the feeling that something was wrong.

Twenty-Eight
Abby

I closed up at the café shortly after seven and got in my car, debating what to do for dinner. I was too tired to cook anything, and Nate was on shift until tomorrow morning, so it wasn't like I could convince him to come hang out and order a pizza with me. I could order one for myself, but I felt guilty, knowing I would eat the whole thing and then regret it later.

Instead, I drove the short distance across town to the Surf 'N Shack and waited in the long line that wound outside and around the building. It was the best place to get fish and chips, and I had yet to find the perfect time to come when there wasn't a line.

My feet hurt, but I ignored their protests and shifted my weight, knowing it would be worth the pain to get food here. My stomach growled in excitement, my mouth already salivating as the aroma floated through the doors as a handful of lucky bastards came out with their to-go bags of deliciousness.

The line moved quickly, and soon I was inside, out of the cold. I looked around, my stomach somersaulting when I spotted Colin sitting at one of the tables across the room from me with a guy that we went to school with.

I looked away quickly, hoping that he hadn't noticed me, but felt the heat prickle down my neck as I caught him walking my way out of the corner of my eye.

"Hey, Abby," he said casually when he reached me. "Seems we can't stop running into each other today."

I laughed nervously, then scratched at my neck.

"Well, technically, I was supposed to be at work, and you were the one who just showed up out of the blue."

His brows jumped up as he rubbed his lips together to keep from laughing. As much as he didn't change since high school, apparently, I hadn't either because he could still easily tell how awkward and uncomfortable I was right now.

"Sorry, I guess I should have called and given you a heads up," he said lightly.

He had changed out of the polo and trousers that he was wearing this morning and now had on a hoodie with dark denim jeans that seemed to show off his ass. Not that I was checking it out.

Okay—so I was. But you can't blame me—the thing was plump and tight enough that you could bounce a quarter off of it. Plus, I had all of these damned pregnancy hormones rushing through me that forced me to notice things like this—as guilty as I felt about it afterward.

"How did you like my muffin?" I blurted out, trying to change the conversation but only making it worse.

"It was good, I really enjoyed it. Thank you."

I chewed the inside of my cheek and looked away as we stepped forward to move with the line.

"So, how have you been?" he asked, his body totally relaxed and opposite of mine.

I subconsciously rubbed a hand across my stomach, wondering how I should explain it when I saw his eyes trail over my bump. Instead of the fear I saw in Vince's eyes when I told him that I was pregnant, I saw something different in Colin's.

"I've been good," I replied softly, thankful that my nerves were slowly starting to calm down. "Really good."

"You look good. Happy."

"I am."

We moved forward again, getting closer to the front of the line when I felt my phone vibrate in my pocket. I pulled it out and saw a text message from Nate but didn't open it, suddenly feeling rude and overly guilty for talking to Colin while carrying Nate's baby.

"Is that your husband?" he asked, nodding to the phone I shoved back into my pocket.

"No," I shook my head. "I'm not married."

My nerves were skyrocketing again as I felt a bead of sweat trickle down the back of my neck. Thankfully my hair was longer now and could hide it.

"I'm not even engaged," I laughed. "Just having a baby with my best friend." I rocked back on my heels and gave him the most awkward smile.

I waited for him to turn and bolt, but his smile grew wider across his face.

"Hey, Abby?"

"Yeah?"

"You don't have to be so nervous around me. I'm not here to judge you or anything you've done with your life. On the contrary, I think it's wonderful that you're getting the life you've always dreamed of. Your happiness is all that anyone should ever want for you."

My heart started racing as I had a million flashbacks to the days when I would lay curled up against him, and he would offer me words of encouragement when I needed it.

"Thank you," I whispered softly, finally feeling some of the anxiety lift.

We were next in line when I felt a sudden sharp pain in my stomach. I hunched over and grabbed my side, groaning as another one shot through me.

"Woah," he said, placing his hand on my lower back and reaching forward to hold my hand that was still rubbing my stomach. "Are you okay?"

I stood upright as he watched me, arms ready to catch me if I were to fall.

"Yeah, I think so," I replied with uncertainty.

"Next," the woman at the register called.

We walked over to the counter when another pain coursed through me, nearly making my knees buckle.

"I think we need to get you to the hospital," he said calmly.

"But my food," I objected, looking desperately at the cashier.

Before I could place my order, I felt another one and knew that he was right. I had no idea what contractions felt like, but my guess was that these weren't simple hunger pains.

With tears in my eyes, we turned and left the restaurant as he helped me into his car and drove me to the hospital.

Twenty-Nine
Nate

It was after nine, and I still hadn't heard from Abby. I had sent a few text messages to check on her but hadn't heard anything. Finally, I decided to give in and call her. I hoped that she hadn't fallen asleep because I would hate to wake her up, but I also hated not knowing if she was okay.

Her phone rang six times before it was answered. However, instead of hearing Abby's voice, I heard a man's.

"Abby's phone," they said softly into the phone.

"Who's this?" I asked, sitting up straight on the bed.

"Hey, Nate, it's Colin. I'm with Abby."

I bit the inside of my lip to keep from saying something rude. I knew that he was back in town and that it was only a matter of time before she ran into him. I guess I just expected her to tell me about it first and not have him answer her phone after giving me the silent treatment all night.

"Hey."

"Hold on a minute, let me step out of the room so we can talk," he said.

Out of the room? What the fuck had they been doing?

I was about to hang up the phone when he came back onto the line.

"I'm glad you called, I was just getting ready to reach out to you. Abby is in the hospital. We just got here about twenty minutes ago. Everything's okay, she'll be checked by the doctor again here in a bit."

My heart sank, and I clutched the phone tighter.

"What happened?" Was all that I was able to get out.

"She started having contractions, and they've given her medicine to try to stop them. They're monitoring her now, and the baby is doing fine. Her contractions have slowed down, but they want to keep her a little longer since they haven't completely stopped."

"Okay, I'm on my way."

"See you soon."

I hung up and jumped off of the bed. I hated that she was in the hospital and I didn't know it. But what was even worse was that he was there with her, and I wasn't.

Twenty minutes later, I was rushing through the hallways of the hospital, looking for the room Abby was in. Finally, I spotted Colin standing outside and walked over to him.

"How's she doing?" I asked, looking past him, but the door was closed.

"She's tired and pissed off that she didn't get dinner, but other than that, she's good. Doctor Nicoli is with her now."

I let out the breath I was holding and leaned against the wall beside him.

"Thank you for letting me know what was going on," I said, glancing at him.

"Not a problem. Like I said, I was just getting ready to call you when you called. I would have called when we were on the way, but she was in so much pain that I couldn't focus on anything other than getting her here."

I nodded and looked straight ahead at the stark white wall in front of me.

"Where were you guys?" I asked, wondering if I really wanted to know.

"I ran into her at the Surf 'N Shack. I was meeting a friend for drinks, and she was there to get dinner. We were talking while she waited in line, then the contractions started. I didn't even think, I just brought her straight here. Sorry if I overstepped."

I turned to look at him, wondering what all he knew about the current situation between Abby and me.

"You didn't overstep at all. I'm glad you were there and that you got her here."

"I'm happy for you guys," he said softly. "I know I've been gone for a long time, but I can't honestly say I've ever seen Abby this happy." He paused, then winced when he added, "well, she was happy until we had to leave before she got her food."

I let my head fall back and let out a laugh.

"Yeah, she gets hangry real quick these days."

"She threatened to stab me in the eye with a rusty fork on our way to the hospital if I didn't turn around and take her back to get her fish and chips.”

“Last week, I accidentally ate the last Oreo, and she gave me the silent treatment for the rest of the day. I went to get breakfast the next day at Rockin’ Rooster, and she refused to serve me.”

“Yikes.”

“Yeah, I still haven’t gotten fully back into her good graces yet.”

“Did you buy more Oreos?” he asked, turning to smile at me.

“I bought her three packs. She hid them throughout her house and won’t tell me where they are. I had to buy my own pack and share with her.”

We were both laughing when the door opened, and Doctor Nicoli stepped out.

“Abby is doing well, and the contractions have stopped. I want to keep her for a few more hours to ensure they don’t start up again. If all is well, then she can be released. I strongly advise that she rests as much as possible for the next few days,” he said after shaking my hand.

“The holiday festival starts tomorrow, and she’s planning to work their booth,” I said with a heavy sigh.

“Yeah, she told me. I know that I can’t talk her out of it, but I’m hoping that she can rest there as much as possible. I worry that she will end up back in here if not.”

“I’ll talk to her. Maybe I can get her to agree to rest instead.”

Doctor Nicoli smiled at us and then excused himself to check on another patient. I knew that getting Abby to miss the festival would be damn near impossible, but I also knew how much this baby meant to her.

I entered the room with Colin right behind me. Abby looked up, a surprised look on her face when she found us together.

"Oh, hey," she said quietly. "Sorry I didn't call you…"

"You were dealing with more important stuff." I went over and squeezed her hand, making sure she really was okay. "How are you feeling?"

"Better now that the contractions have stopped. Man, those things were painful. I'm not looking forward to when labor really starts."

Colin and I smiled, probably both feeling bad that we had no idea how much pain she had been in nor the amount of pain she would face in labor.

"Is there anything I can do for you?" I offered, taking the seat next to her bed while Colin took the other.

"Unless you can get me my food from Surf 'N Shack, I'm good."

I checked my watch, confirming they were already closed. I grimaced and avoided looking at her for a few seconds so I didn't have to see the disappointment on her face.

"How about I pick up lunch from there tomorrow, then we can have a movie marathon and binge-watch some Christmas movies?"

She pulled her brows together and folded her arms over her chest.

"I have the holiday festival tomorrow, Nate. You know that."

"Yes," I sighed. "And you know that Doctor Nicoli recommended that you stay home and rest so you don't end up back in the hospital again."

Her face fell, and she rubbed her hand over her stomach. I reached for it, wanting to touch her and hoping the baby would greet me with a kick when I noticed Colin looking away. Even though it had been almost twenty years since he left, I had no idea if he still had feelings for Abby and whether that was the reason he was suddenly back.

"He talked to you?"

I nodded.

"He updated me in the hallway. And I know that you hate to miss it, but I also know how much this baby means to you, and I think you should consider resting for a few days. Maybe you can go on Sunday, so you don't have to miss the whole thing?"

"But if I don't go tomorrow, they'll be short-handed. It's the first day, which is always the busiest, and I don't have anyone to cover for me. It wouldn't be fair for me to do that to them."

"Abby, it's not fair to put your health at risk either," I countered. I understood what she was saying, but it didn't make it any easier for me to dismiss that she might be risking the baby's health too.

"What other options do I have? It's not like I want to end up back in the hospital, but I also have a responsibility to—"

"I'll cover for you," Colin offered, pulling both of our

attention to him.

"What?" Abby blurted out in surprise.

"I'll cover for you. I know most of the locals, so they'll take pity on me not knowing what I'm doing, and I'm great at taking direction, so I'm sure your team can get me caught up on whatever I need to know."

"Colin, you don't have to do that. You should spend your time with…."

"It's fine, I really don't mind. Plus, I have plenty of time to spend with my family now that I'm back for good."

My brows rose involuntarily as I took in that tidbit of information.

"Are you sure?" she asked, a hint of doubt lingering in her voice.

"Absolutely."

Her shoulders relaxed with the sigh that escaped past her lips as she leaned back in the bed and rubbed her stomach.

"But I do have a favor that I'll need from you later," he added with a wink.

And that was when I knew the other shoe was about to drop.

Thirty
Abby

"Do you remember that time that you went down on me for like two hours, and I came four times?" I asked Nate as I shoved the last bite into my mouth and chewed.

He smiled a cheeky grin and nodded.

"This is *almost* as good as that," I sighed, taking a drink of water. "And we both know how fucking fantastic that night was."

"Good to know," he laughed. "If I ever need to get in your good graces, I'll get you take out from Surf 'N Shack and then go down on you while you devour some fish and chips."

The heat prickled my cheeks as I blushed, thinking with way too much detail about how wonderful that would be.

"Do you want more?" he offered, lifting his box toward me. While I could definitely keep eating, I was full and didn't want to be uncomfortable. Plus, I didn't want to always be stealing his food.

"I'm good, but thank you. And thank you again for picking up lunch, it was delicious."

"You're very welcome. I'm glad you enjoyed it. What movie do you want to watch next?"

I knew he was doing everything in his power to make me happy today, but I couldn't shake how disappointed I was that I didn't get to be at the holiday festival today. It was an annual tradition, which made Christmas feel even less normal than before. Between my parents being gone and missing the festival, I found it hard to get in the holiday spirit this year.

"We don't have to watch anything," I said bitterly, pushing myself off the couch to throw away our trash. It was getting harder to get up, and I hated that I looked like a whale when I still had three months to grow. How huge was I going to get?

Nate followed me into the kitchen and helped clean up the mess before he wrapped me in a hug and held me.

"I know this is frustrating, how can I help?"

"There's nothing that will help," I muttered against his chest. "Everything is different and I'm just not feeling Christmas this year. It's fine, though. Really."

He leaned back and lifted my chin with his finger.

"Abby, you love Christmas. I know this one feels harder, but we can still make it amazing."

I pulled back, shook my head, and bit the inside of my cheek as I tried to force the tears away.

I didn't want Nate to work so hard at cheering me up. It wasn't his job to make sure that I was happy, even though I appreciated him trying. But this time, it would take a miracle to pull me out of this funk I was in, and it wasn't fair to him to carry that burden.

I turned and put the rest of the food in the fridge, thankful that Nate had bought extra so I didn't have to cook dinner tonight either. It was likely that he would still be here and would end up cooking because he didn't like to eat out that often, but I didn't want to count on it.

When I finished, I found him leaning against the wall with a smile as he did something on his phone.

"What are you so happy about?" I asked, feeling the corners of my lips turn up to mimic his.

"I have a surprise. Go take a shower and get dressed."

"Why? Where are we going?"

"It wouldn't be a surprise if I told you, now would it? But rest assured, you won't be on your feet, and I guarantee you're going to stay resting." He winked and kissed the top of my head before going to the living room and plopping down on the couch.

I felt a tiny spark of joy at the idea of him planning something for me and couldn't wait to see what it was. I took a quick shower, making sure that I wasn't on my feet longer than necessary. Once I was done, I got dressed in a comfy cotton dress that I had been wanting to wear and matched it to a pair of maternity leggings that had recently become my best friend. I sat on my bed, putting on my makeup while my hair dried, then I was ready for whatever he had lined up for us.

He was smiling in the car as we drove, and I felt the excitement start to spread over me. I loved seeing him happy, and it made me feel special that I was the reason for the smile on his face right now—that doing something to make me happy had created so much happiness for him.

We turned into the parking lot of the community center, and I felt my heart sink a little.

"What are we doing here?" I asked, the sadness washing over me in waves.

"I know how much it means to you to be here," he said, coming around to help me get out of the car.

"But it's not fair to my team that I called in because I'm supposed to be resting, then I show up and walk around. I don't know that it's a good idea to be on my feet that long."

"I know," he said, moving to the side while I stayed sitting in the car. Suddenly Capshaw appeared out of nowhere with a wheelchair that he parked beside the car.

"I've already talked to Tom and Cindy, they're excited to see you and wanted me to assure you that they have everything under control. Apparently, Colin has been the biggest rock star and has totally jumped right in and has been a godsend. We had an extra wheelchair at the station that we don't need, so Capshaw went and got it for us."

"Nate," I whispered, unable to believe what he was saying. "You didn't have to do that."

He leaned in and kissed me softly.

"I wanted to."

Thirty-One
Nate

I wheeled Abby around, stopping at the different tables as we said hi to everyone and browsed the items they had for sale. I loved how her eyes lit up with joy from being there and knew that I had made the right call today. When we got to the Rockin' Rooster booth in the corner, we watched Colin take the lead, acting like he belonged there as he cleared the line in a matter of minutes.

"Do you think I should offer him a job," Abby whispered to me out of the side of her mouth as we got closer.

I chuckled while I worked to fight off the jealousy that poked its ugly head through at the thought of them working together every day. I knew I had nothing to be jealous of, but that didn't stop it from festering every chance it had.

It had only been a few days since he had come back to town, and since then, he'd been nothing but helpful where Abby was concerned. I wanted to hate him for leaving town and crushing Abby's heart, but if she could forgive him—which it seemed like she had—then why should I keep a grudge? It wasn't like it was *my* heart he broke.

I pushed the wheelchair up to the table, and she squealed in happiness as Cindy told her how well the day had gone. Colin leaned back against the wall, out of the way, while they talked. I admired that he didn't feel the need to step in and boast about how helpful he had been. It seemed as though he genuinely wanted to help and wasn't doing it just for attention or to impress Abby.

"That's amazing!" Abby said, shifting in the chair. "I'm so sorry that I had to miss it today."

"Please don't worry about it," Tom assured her. "We've been just fine, and Colin has been nothing but helpful."

"Are we hiring? Because I think he needs a job *ASAP*!" Cindy said, trying to be quiet but anyone in a three-foot radius could hear her—including Colin. Her skin blushed as she glanced behind her to find his eyes on her, giving me a sense of hope that maybe there was something there between them.

"I'm not sure, but we can definitely look into it," Abby answered, looking past Tom and Cindy to Colin. As if sensing this was his cue, he pushed off of the wall and joined the rest of them.

"How are you feeling?" he asked, his eyes soft as he smiled at her.

"A lot better than yesterday, thanks for asking."

"Did you get your fish and chips?" He raised a brow and looked at me with a knowing smile.

I placed my hands on her shoulders and gently squeezed.

"She sure did," I replied, trying to keep the smug smile at bay as I thought about her comment earlier. Going down on Abby while she was eating wasn't anything new, and now I was determined to make sure her next orgasm was better than anything she would ever get at Surf 'N Shack.

"We're going to keep shopping, but I'll stop by again before we go," Abby said, interrupting my dirty thoughts.

I smiled at everyone as I turned her around and headed in the other direction. The holiday festival was always busy, but this year it felt like there were more people here than usual. There were also more vendors than any year before, some coming from neighboring towns which wasn't uncommon. I imagined that was also where the influx of visitors came from as well.

We browsed and stocked up on plenty of sweets while Abby finished her shopping. I knew that it was hard for her to buy gifts for her parents, knowing that they wouldn't get to open them for a few months when they got back from their trip. She reached for a box of peanut brittle and then put it back. After that, she grabbed a box of gourmet chocolates, frowned, and put it back as well.

"You know, most of that stuff has a decent shelf life," I said, nodding to the food items she had set down. "They would still be good by the time they got back."

She sighed and looked up at me.

"I know, I just feel weird buying them Christmas gifts when they're not going to open them until March. I feel like I should be getting a bunch of green stuff with shamrocks."

"Well, I mean, we can go hard for St. Patrick's day this year if you want to," I teased with a grin.

She playfully nudged me in the side.

"Very funny. Why is this so hard?"

"Because change is hard."

She rubbed her stomach and shifted in her seat. I could tell that it was starting to get uncomfortable for her to sit so long without any decent padding. She ended up buying the brittle and assorted chocolates, and then we made our way through the last few aisles. Once we were done, her lap was piled with bags while she tried to hold them without letting any fall.

An hour later, we said our goodbyes and drove back to her place. I helped her get everything inside while she went to the bathroom to pee again. I wasn't sure if she wanted me to stay or if she wanted some alone time, so I lingered in the kitchen, pretending to organize her bags until she was done.

I heard her footsteps as she waddled into the room. While she would punch me for saying that she waddled, I found it absolutely adorable and loved the sound of it.

"Whatcha doing?" she asked, wrapping her arms around my waist while cuddling her tummy to my back.

The baby promptly kicked me, telling me not to touch their mom.

"Just making sure nothing fell before you could unpack it."

"So kind of you," she murmured as she stood on her tiptoes and planted kisses along the back of my neck.

I turned around and wrapped my arms around her. She bit her lip, her brown eyes darkening slightly.

"What can I say? I'm a kind guy."

"Is that so?" She tilted her head and locked eyes with me as she lifted the bottom of my shirt and pushed it up to my chest.

She leaned forward and planted kisses along my abs, letting her tongue leave a trail of fire while my cock hardened in my jeans. I closed my eyes and let my hand run through her hair as she kept going. Her fingers quickly worked my belt before unbuttoning my jeans and lowering my zipper.

I felt Abby slide down my body as she attempted to get on her knees, and my eyes flew open as I reached out to stop her. Not that I didn't want a blow job from Abby, but there was no way in hell that I was going to let her get on her knees for me when she was six months pregnant.

My hands held her elbows and lifted her back up.

"You don't want me to?" she asked, the rejection heavy in her voice.

"Of course I do, but I'm not letting you get on your knees in the middle of the kitchen when you're pregnant."

"I'm fine," she insisted, reaching for me again.

"I would feel better if we did this in your room, on your comfortable—and padded—bed."

She looked like she was going to argue with me for a moment before she sighed and shrugged her shoulders as she turned and headed for the room. I followed behind her like a desperate dog about to get a treat.

Abby was already waiting for me and standing at the edge of the bed when I nodded for her to get on it. She rolled her eyes and started climbing up when I stopped her.

"Did you just roll your eyes at me?" I asked, holding onto her arm while desire rushed through me. I knew that this role-playing was a huge turn-on for her ever since she started reading lines to me from the books she was reading. While I read everything I needed to know about parenting for dummies, Abby had been focused on *other* types of books. But hell, I wasn't complaining because they made her super horny, and she was willing to try most of the stuff she read about.

"No, sir," she said, shaking her head slightly while her eyes lit up.

I raised my brow and slid my belt through the loops, watching her face as it swooshed through the air.

"I'll ask again—did you roll your eyes at me? Bad girls get punished, Abby."

She swallowed hard, her eyes focused on the belt as I held it folded in one hand, ready to snap it at any moment.

"I'm sorry, sir."

"Strip off your clothes," I commanded. "Then get on the bed."

She did as instructed and waited for me, naked and ready for me to ravage her on the bed.

I slowly undressed, loving the way she looked as she watched me. Her nipples hardened, and I knew that if I were to slip a finger between her thighs, I would feel the heat from her pussy.

Once I was undressed, I leisurely stroked my cock and walked over to the bed.

"Is this what you want?" I asked, looking down at my erection as I squeezed it tightly.

She nodded, eager to rush over to me.

"Tell me," I commanded. "What do you want, Abby?"

She swallowed, then pulled her shoulders back, putting her plump tits on display for me. They had grown significantly with pregnancy, and I couldn't wait for the opportunity to slide my dick between them if she would let me.

"I want to suck your cock," she breathed. I raised my brows, and she continued. "Sir."

"As you wish," I said, letting my hand drop from it as she crawled over and grabbed it.

It was the perfect sight as she bent in front of me, legs spread apart on the bed while she used one hand to balance herself and the other to stroke me while she took me all the way to the back of her throat. She looked at me under thick eyelashes as she bobbed up and down, making me feel incredible.

I closed my eyes and held her head in place as she continued her magic on my cock. She shifted her position without taking her mouth off of me. I opened my eyes to make sure she was okay when I heard a loud noise rumble past me.

She pulled away immediately, her face reddening by the second. As quickly as she could, she jumped off the bed and ran to the bathroom. The door slammed behind her while I stood there with a hard cock in a room that smelled like rotten eggs. It was true—pregnancy farts were worse than regular ones.

Thirty-Two
Abby

I farted. I totally farted in the middle of giving Nate a blow job. Now, while I could argue that farting was technically *blowing,* we both knew that it wasn't at all what he had in mind when I offered him one. This suddenly gave new meaning to *Project Abby Blows.*

I slid down onto the toilet and covered my face with my hands. I had done plenty of embarrassing things in front of Nate before, but this far exceeded everything else. If he never wanted to speak to me again, I wouldn't blame him.

The worst part was that it wasn't just an innocent little fart—it was loud and disgusting. I told him that being pregnant made everything worse, and now, unfortunately, he would know that I wasn't lying.

And the worst part of all this was that I had locked myself in my bathroom—naked—while I tried to figure out how to save face. It wasn't like I could send him a text and pretend I wasn't feeling well so he would leave. I didn't have my phone, and even if I did, I doubted he would listen.

I sat there for a few minutes, trying to figure out my next move when I heard a knock on the door.

"You can't stay in there forever," he said softly.

"Wanna bet?"

"There's no food in there. You'll eventually have to come out to eat."

I looked around helplessly.

"There's soap. I can eat that and pray that it cleans out my system."

He laughed on the other side, and I was slightly relieved that he found some humor in all of this.

"I don't think that's how it works."

"We won't know until we try."

"I love you, Abby, but I gotta admit—I don't think I want to be part of that experiment."

I cringed and lowered my head to my chest as I tried to keep from laughing.

"Open the door and come out. I won't bite."

I glanced at the door and considered it. If he wasn't making a big deal about it, why should I? It was a natural—yet gross—thing that everyone did. Being pregnant just made it harder to keep them in until I could get to the privacy of my bathroom. It wasn't like I was some sort of monster who did it to him on purpose.

I stood up and sucked in a deep breath, wrapping a towel around me before opening the door.

Nate stood in front of me, wearing my bra as a face mask.

"I wasn't sure if the chemical warfare was over."

I shook my head and pursed my lips.

"You're terrible," I teased, pushing past him to the bedroom so I could retrieve the rest of my clothes.

He had his briefs on—as well as my bra that was still covering his mouth—but aside from that, he was still naked. I reached for my panties when he stopped me.

"We don't have to do anything," I muttered, refusing to look at him.

"We never *have* to. That doesn't mean that I don't want to."

I continued to look away from him, still embarrassed by what had happened.

"What can I do to make you feel more comfortable?" he asked, wrapping his arms around me. "If you really don't want to do anything, that's fine too. I won't pressure you, but I don't want you to stop because you got embarrassed."

"I'm still embarrassed," I laughed nervously, letting him pull me into his body while he trailed kisses down the side of my neck.

"Don't be. I'm not bothered by it, you shouldn't be either."

"It was gross."

"But it's over, and now we can move on. And trust me, I'd like to move on," he joked as he pushed his erection against my ass.

I closed my eyes and moaned, feeling the ache build between my thighs again.

"What position would make you feel comfortable?"

I didn't have to think hard about it. I knew I wanted to try something that I recently read in a book but hadn't brought up to him until now. Not to say that I hadn't been planning for this moment when I picked up some supplies in Ocean City last week when I went to wrap up what I could of my Christmas shopping.

"Anything?" I asked, trying to feel him out.

He slipped his hand into my towel and untucked it, letting it pool around my feet on the floor.

"Whatever you want, Abby." He playfully nipped my earlobe as he slipped a hand between my thighs.

I felt dizzy from his touch and didn't think through my answer before responding with, "I want you to fuck me in the ass."

He pulled his hand away and spun me around to face him. I felt the heat prickle my cheeks as I stared at him, wondering what was going through his mind as his eyes narrowed at me.

"Did you just say you wanted anal?"

I nodded, pulling my bottom lip between my teeth.

"Like, in the ass?"

I continued nodding, hoping that he didn't say no. I mean, I couldn't blame him if he did; I knew that it wasn't everyone's thing. Heck, I should have tried it years ago when I was young and free, but being super horny all the time and reading about it in my books had sparked a curiosity that I wanted to explore *before* the baby got here.

He ran a hand through his hair and looked around the room before looking at me again.

"It's fine if you don't want to," I rushed out, then stopped when he lifted his hand to stop me.

"I want to," he replied quickly. "Trust me, *I want to*. I just never thought that you would be interested in it."

"I've never tried it, but I read about it in a book," I shrugged.

He grabbed me and pulled me into his chest, gripping my ass as he held me. A wicked smile pulled up the corners of his lips.

"Remind me to buy you more books. All of the books, Abby—they're yours if they spur these kinds of ideas in you," he growled.

I giggled as he slapped my ass and brought his mouth down to gently cover mine.

We kissed for a few minutes, then he pulled away and held my head between his hands.

"Are you sure about this?"

"I'm sure. I haven't done it before, but I thought we could figure it out together."

He licked his lips, then worked his jaw back and forth a few times as if deciding how to tell me something.

"I've actually done it before," he said easily.

"You have?" My eyebrows rose in surprise.

He nodded but didn't offer any other information. Just because Nate and I had been best friends our entire lives didn't mean that we had shared all of the nitty-gritty details about our sex lives over the years. I shared those secrets with Jane, and I guess I had always assumed guys just didn't talk about that stuff, or he talked about it with the guys at the fire station.

"Don't worry, you're in good hands," he assured me.

I knew that he said *not* to worry, but I instantly started to. He made it seem like there was a lot to know about it, and I wondered just how painful it might be. The woman in my book seemed to enjoy it, but then again, she was a fictional character and probably felt pain the same way the guy who had been shot in the stomach two chapters before felt pain as he walked around and saved her from the bad guys. Not to mention he still had the strength to fuck her in the ass WITH a gunshot wound. Perhaps I had been a bit too trusting in the latest mafia romance I had picked up.

My mind was racing, my thoughts going a mile a minute as I thought about everything that could possibly go wrong. *Would it somehow hurt the baby? Was it safe to do anal when you were pregnant? Would I fart again?*

Nate watched me from across the room while he lit a few candles and arranged pillows on the bed. I had shown him the supplies I picked up, which he seemed to approve of as he took them from me and set them on the nightstand.

I was tired from standing, so I went over and sat on the edge of the bed, not bothered about being naked and on full display. I mean, I had already farted while in the middle of giving him a blow job—what else could be more embarrassing than that?

He turned the TV on, and a few minutes later, he was controlling it with his phone. I was still going through the list of things that could go wrong when I heard moaning and looked up to find a woman on the TV with a man taking her from behind.

My nipples hardened as I watched them. I had forgotten for a brief moment that Nate was still in the room until he crawled across the bed behind me and started kissing the back of my neck.

"Scoot back on the bed," he instructed softly, moving so I had room.

I found the pile of pillows he had lined up and eyed them suspiciously.

"We'll get to that if and when you're ready. For now, why don't you get comfortable?"

I smiled and tried to shake off the nerves.

I crawled up to the head of the bed and sat beside Nate, thankful that he had taken his briefs off again. We both leaned against the headboard and watched the couple on the TV as he wrapped her hair around his fist and pulled her head back while he continued to thrust inside of her.

"Which one turns you on more?" Nate asked, his fingers lightly trailing up my thigh.

I shifted on the bed, spreading my legs slightly to allow him to slip one inside of me.

"The girl," I answered breathlessly.

Just then, another man came on the screen and stood in front of her, stroking his cock as she eagerly watched him. I couldn't hear much over her moaning and the sound of blood rushing past my ears, but apparently, he asked her if she wanted his cock because a few seconds later, he was sliding it into her mouth.

My legs spread wider as the ache grew. Nate inserted another finger, spreading my lips as he fucked me in tune with the couple on TV. I continued to watch as he leaned over and pulled a nipple into his mouth, sucking hard while his thumb rubbed my clit.

I let out a loud moan and closed my eyes as he sent me over the edge. I came hard on his fingers, my body spasming in joy. Once I was finished, I looked over to find him stroking his cock while he watched me.

"Fuck me, Nate," I begged, getting up and climbing over to the pillows. "Now."

"Patience, Abby," he laughed. "You don't want to rush this—trust me."

My body was on fire, and right now, I wanted to rush everything. I wanted to ride him more than all of the rides that came with an unlimited ride pass at the state fair.

I waited while he helped me line the pillows up under my stomach and got into the position he guided me to. We were both turned on and ready, so I couldn't imagine there was much left to do at this point.

He grabbed the bottle of lube from the nightstand and flipped open the cap. I turned around and looked, curious to see what he was doing.

I expected him to slather his dick in it, but instead, he squirted some in his hand and then rubbed it on my ass, focusing on the puckered hole that suddenly felt shy to have him anywhere near it.

"Relax," he said softly, his fingers gently smoothing the lube around me. "You have to stay relaxed for me, okay? You can't tense up."

"Okay," I breathed, sucking in a breath as I felt his finger push into me.

"Remember to breathe," he instructed. "I need to get you ready for me first, and that means that I'm going to insert a finger inside of your ass. Once you adjust to that, I'll add another. After that, we'll keep going until you're ready for my cock."

I nodded and tried to relax against the pillows as he rubbed the lube around me. He had one finger fully inside of me, pushing it in and out while squirting more lube into his other hand. I took slow, deep breaths as I got used to the feeling, then sucked in another deep breath when I felt another finger slide inside.

It was painful each time, but after a few seconds, the pain subsided, and it started to feel good. Nate was a couple of fingers in when I closed my eyes and enjoyed the feel of him as he fucked my ass with his fingers.

"Are you ready for me?" he asked, his voice strained and gruff.

"Yes," I whimpered, not entirely sure I was, but it felt too good to stop now.

I felt the absence of his fingers as he pulled them out. He squirted more lube onto my ass and then more into his hand. I glanced over my shoulder to see him coating his dick in it. He wiped his hands on the towel he brought in when he was preparing, then gripped my hips as he held the tip of his cock against my asshole.

I watched the couple on TV as she slid onto one guy and got into position before another guy mounted her from behind. My jaw dropped as she took both guys at the same time, feeling completely turned on and wondering if it was something that Nate would ever be interested in—not that I had another guy in mind to join us.

Before I could overthink it, I felt more pressure against my asshole and knew that it was going to happen.

"Are you ready?" he asked, pausing as he waited for me to confirm.

"Yes," I answered, turning my head so he could hear me.

Slowly he pushed inside me, and I felt the same burning sensation as before. I clenched and bent my head down as I tried to catch my breath.

"You have to remember to relax and breathe, Abby," he coaxed as he rubbed my back. "If you don't want to do this, we don't have to."

"I want it," I assured him, lowering my belly back onto the pillow as I took a calming breath. "Just go slow, okay?"

"Absolutely."

I continued to inhale through my nose and exhale slowly through my mouth as he pushed a little bit further, then stopped to let me get used to him.

The burning stopped almost as quickly as it had before, and I was relieved that it felt even better than his fingers had.

"You can control it," he offered, holding onto my hips.

I nodded and gently started to move, rocking my hips as I felt him tighten behind me.

"Is that okay?" I asked, not sure if it felt good for him.

"It's fucking perfect," he breathed.

"You can take over," I said. "I don't mind. It doesn't hurt anymore. It feels good."

He grunted as he started thrusting. It wasn't hard or painful like I had expected. Instead, it was the perfect combination of hard and fast, and before I knew it, he was coming inside me. I smiled, wondering when we would be able to do this again.

Thirty-Three
Nate

Saturday morning, I got up and made breakfast for Abby before heading to Ocean City to pick up her Christmas gift. I hadn't decided if I wanted to give it to her on Wednesday, which was Christmas Eve or add it to the things I had lined up for her on Christmas Day.

She was putzing around the house for the day, which gave me an opportunity to get out and run my errands. Part of me knew that she was trying to get me out of the house as well because she kept insisting that she was tired and fake yawning.

The drive to Ocean City was peaceful and allowed me time to think. Not that I had a lot on my mind, but more so that I couldn't stop obsessing over last night. When Abby asked me to fuck her in the ass, my jaw dropped while my cock throbbed at the thought of being her first anal experience. I loved that she trusted me enough to experience that with me, but more so that she initiated the conversation about it. Anal was by far my favorite, but I would never have approached her about it on my own.

I pulled into the parking lot and got out, excited to see the gift I had custom-made for her. The last time I was here, I found this little shop that restored old photos and snuck Abby's favorite photo album out of her house when she wasn't looking. There were pictures of her with her grandparents when she was little, as well as some from school that I wanted to put into an album for the baby of how mommy and daddy met.

"Hello, I'm here to pick up an order," I said to the woman at the front desk.

"Oh, yes," she smiled, her hazel eyes lighting up when she looked at me. "I just finished it yesterday, dear."

She got up and grabbed her walker, making her way to another counter where a box was wrapped with a beautiful gold bow.

"I haven't finished wrapping it yet so you could check everything first, but if you like it, I can go ahead and wrap it for you before you go."

"Thank you," I said, taking it from her and following her over to the small table against the back wall and sitting down.

I lifted the lid and reached inside, pulling out the first album that was a custom one she had made for me. Since we didn't know if the baby was a boy or a girl, we agreed to do an ivory color with a picture of the baby's first ultrasound in the pocket on the front cover.

I thumbed through the pages, smiling as I looked at the years that had passed between Abby and me. The last few pages had pictures of us that I had taken recently, as well as some of Abby that she had never seen before. Whenever I could, I snapped photos of her growing belly and captured the moments when she thought no one was looking.

My eyes locked onto the photo of Abby staring down at her stomach on Thanksgiving, her hand placed lovingly on it while the most beautiful smile graced her face. The baby had been kicking non-stop after she ate the pie she had made from her grandma's recipe that she had written down before she passed.

"This is beautiful," I whispered, covering my mouth with my hand to hold the emotion inside.

"I really enjoyed making that one. Such a beautiful couple." She smiled at the picture of Abby and me that Jane had taken last week. We both looked deliriously happy as she looked up at me, and I grinned down at her while wrapping my hands around her stomach.

"Thank you." I didn't correct her that we weren't a couple. For just one moment, I wanted to pretend that we were; that Abby was mine, and that we were starting our family and living happily ever after.

Thirty-Four
Abby

By Sunday, my feet were still swollen, and no matter how much I wanted to get off my ass and make it to the holiday festival, I couldn't. I felt terrible that I had to miss this year, but even worse, I was constantly letting my team down.

I asked Cindy if she could cover again, and while she was hesitant at first, she quickly perked up and volunteered when she found out that Colin was going to be there. I tried not to feel a little possessive of him, but it was weird to see another woman so desperate for his attention. I wondered if he felt the same way about her, then remembered that it wasn't any of my damn business.

Things with Colin ended almost twenty years ago. It wasn't like he was just going to waltz back into my life, and we would pick up where we left off. No matter how much in love we thought we were back then, that didn't mean that that kind of love could survive almost twenty years of being apart. Hell, we had both changed dramatically during that time and weren't even the same people anymore.

I picked up my phone to check for any urgent messages and felt disappointed when everyone confirmed they were doing just fine without me. Cindy and Colin were handling the festival just fine, and Sherry was working with Tom at Rockin' Rooster and didn't need any help either.

Feeling unwanted and more importantly—unneeded—I got up and grabbed the wrapping paper and tape from the counter, then went in search of the gifts that I had hidden throughout the house. If I didn't get a head start on wrapping them today, I would be rushing to have them done by Wednesday when we were celebrating with Jane and the kids, as well as Nate's parents.

I was just about to sit down to get started when I heard the doorbell ring. I groaned and walked over, wondering who was there when the only person who ever showed up randomly was Nate, and he was busy helping his dad put up lights today. I opened the door and felt a gush of cold air whip past me as Jane rushed in with shopping bags piled up on her arms.

Once she was inside, I shut the door and shivered from the cold she brought in with her.

"It's colder than a witch's tit out there," she mumbled, setting the bags on the counter before shrugging out of her coat.

I nodded, still wondering why she was there.

"The kids are with Rick today, finishing their Christmas shopping," she explained as she grabbed the bags from the counter and took them into the living room. "I needed to finish wrapping mine while they were gone, so I figured I would come over and help you with yours once I'm done."

"How did you know that I hadn't wrapped them yet?" I laughed, plopping down on the couch and knocking half of mine over.

"Because I'm your older sister. I know everything." She winked and sat down on the floor after pushing the coffee table out of the way. "We can work on it together."

I grumbled under my breath and slid off of the couch to the floor.

"Fine," I said with a sigh.

"When we're done, I'll take you for fish and chips at Surf 'N Shack," she sang happily, wiggling her eyebrows as she waved my weakness right in front of me.

I looked down at my pajamas, wondering if it would be worth changing out of them and going out in the cold.

"Alright, alright, we'll have it delivered. But you have to finish yours, and I'll finish mine. Deal?"

"Deal."

We got situated and organized our piles of gifts next to us, then shared the supplies she brought with her, as well as what I already had out. An hour later, we had worked through several piles of gifts that barely made a dent in the stack that still needed to be wrapped.

"How is there *still* so much stuff?" I complained, leaning back against the couch while Jane typed something on her phone.

"We bought a lot of stuff for my kids, and I spoiled my future niece or nephew that hasn't been born yet."

"You know that's what baby showers are supposed to be for?" I joked since she was adamant about throwing me one.

"Eh, you can never have too much baby stuff." She waved her hand dismissively. "Should we keep going?"

"Ugh, do we have to?"

My back ached, and my feet were officially the size of over-inflated balloons.

"Yes, we do. But—we can finish the rest in a bit. Why don't you sit on the couch and take some pressure off your back?"

I nodded, forced myself off the floor, and got comfy while she took the chair opposite me.

"Did you finish shopping for Nate?" she asked, checking her phone.

"I think I'm going to get him one more thing, but I haven't decided what. He's so hard to shop for."

"What have you gotten so far?"

"A few vinyl records he's missing from his collection, a new coffee tumbler that says 'caution—I'm hot', and a few sweaters that I thought would look great on him."

"That's cute," she said, setting her phone down on the armrest beside her. "And I'm surprised to see you buy him clothes when you usually prefer him without." She wiggled her brows suggestively.

My cheeks tinted pink as I thought about Friday night and Nate. What started as an embarrassing disaster quickly turned into one of the hottest nights of my life. Watching porn with him felt totally normal and not at all uncomfortable. And the anal sex—cherry on top.

"Well, it *is* cold outside, and not everyone wants him walking around naked."

"I'm sure plenty of women in town would disagree with that."

I frowned, knowing that was true.

"Hey," she laughed, holding her hands up. "I'm not trying to spoil your fun; I'm just saying that he's still technically one of the few single, eligible bachelors in Beaumont Creek, and women are lined up for their chance with him."

"What am I supposed to do? He hasn't asked me about being his girlfriend and seems content with us just having a baby together and staying best friends. I don't want to risk losing him because I push him into something he doesn't want."

"How do you know that's not what he wants?"

"Wouldn't he have gone for it already if he did?"

"Maybe he's afraid of the same thing—losing you because he pushes too hard and forces you into something you don't want."

"I never said that I didn't want that," I whispered, suddenly feeling vulnerable.

Before we could discuss it any further, the doorbell rang.

Jane got up, clapping her hands as she rushed to the door and opened it. Her smile fell when Capshaw stood on the other side, holding a bag of food.

"What are you doing here?" she asked, hand planted firmly on her hip.

"I was at Surf 'N Shack when your order came in, so I offered to deliver it since they were backed up and short-staffed tonight."

"They just let you take my order?"

"No," he laughed. "It's my family's restaurant. I was there checking on my mom, and she seemed overwhelmed, so I jumped in to help."

"And out of all of the orders, you just somehow ended up with mine?"

"What can I say? I saw an opportunity, so I went for it."

He rocked back on his heels, smiling like a boy on the playground who finally mustered up the courage to talk to his crush.

"You're relentless," she muttered, grabbing her purse from the counter while he propped the door open with his foot. He leaned past her and gave me a quick wave.

"Maybe," he shrugged. "Or just determined."

"Determined?" she asked as she pulled out her wallet and pulled out some cash. "About what?"

"Getting you to go out with me."

She dropped her hand and looked up at him.

"We've been over this, Capshaw. You're just not my type."

He sighed and leaned against the door frame.

"You say that, but I think I could prove you wrong if you gave me a chance."

She glanced at me over her shoulder before turning her attention back to him.

"It's not that easy." Her voice was quiet, but it didn't keep me from noticing how it slightly wavered.

"Here," she said, offering him the cash she had pulled out as a tip.

"No, thank you. It was my pleasure to deliver your food."

He held the bags out to her.

"Capshaw…."

"I don't help out because I need the money, Jane. I do it to help my family."

"Well, thank you."

Jane took the bags from him as he turned to leave.

"Wait," she said, holding up the bags. "It looks like someone else's order might have been added to ours. We only had two orders of chips and fries, but there are three boxes."

He tucked his head and grinned sheepishly.

"I added a few slices of apple pie on the house."

Her eyes went wide as she watched him slightly blush from her attention.

"Why did you do that?"

"I was hoping you would like it. Maybe if you knew that I could bake a wicked pie, you might consider that date with me after all."

He smiled and leaned around her again.

"See you later, Abby."

"Bye, Capshaw."

I couldn't fight the grin that pulled across my face as Jane shut the door behind him, then spun around to look at me with a disheveled look on her face. It took a lot to silence her, and Capshaw had just succeeded with pie.

Thirty-Five
Abby

"What was that?" I asked, joining Jane at the counter where she set the bag of food down.

Technically I wanted to push past her and pry it from her fingers because I was suddenly starving and the smell was overwhelmingly wonderful. But I was a good sister, and that meant I could put my hunger aside for a few minutes to check on my sister, who looked like she had been stunned into silence.

"I don't know," she muttered, blinking her eyes rapidly as if that would force things back into focus.

After taking a few minutes too long to get her shit together, I reached over and pulled the bag from her hands and unpacked the contents. I set the pie to the side, my stomach growling at the heavenly aroma.

"That was weird, right?" she asked, still looking perplexed.

"Kinda. I mean, I had no idea that Capshaw's family owned the Surf 'N Shack. In all honesty, I'm surprised that Nate hasn't brought it up. He just picked up food from there on Friday for us."

"No," she shook her head. "The way he acted. I mean, *who was that?*"

I opened the lid on one of the boxes and felt my mouth salivate in response as I raised a brow at her.

"You mean Capshaw? The guy who has been flirting with you nonstop for how many months now?"

"He hasn't been flirting," she scoffed and picked up her box.

I followed her into the living room and sat on the couch, tucking a pillow under my food before I dove in.

"He's *always* flirting with you."

"No, he's always being obnoxious and rude. But, tonight was… different."

I took a bite and studied her before it dawned on me what was happening.

"You LIKE him!" I shouted, pointing a fry at her. "You totally like him!"

Her face turned beet red as she looked away. We ate silently for a few minutes before she gave in and stubbornly replied, "I do not."

I finished chewing, took a drink of water, then waited for her to look at me again.

"You do too. I can see it written all over your face and by the way you're squirming."

She took a bite and ignored me again.

"It's okay to like him, Jane," I said gently, all of the playful teasing a few minutes ago now gone.

"Oh please," she laughed. "I'm practically old enough to be his mother."

"You're not that much older than he is."

"I'm forty-one, Abby. He's what—twenty-three?"

I tried to remember how old he was, but it wasn't anything that was ever important enough for me to keep track of.

"He's older than that. I think he's in his thirties."

"That's still a ten-year difference."

"So," I shrugged and took another bite. "What difference does it make how old he is?"

"I already have two kids; I don't need another one."

I laughed and snorted, almost choking on a bite of fish.

"You're being ridiculous. It's not the same, and you know it."

"Men in their thirties are immature. I've already seen it from him with his stupid catcalls and hyper-aggressive flirting."

I finished my food and set the empty box on the coffee table.

"You won't know unless you give it a try."

"Now you sound like mom."

"Well, this is one time where that's not a terrible thing. Come on, Jane, it wouldn't hurt you to start dating again. You deserve to be happy."

I got up and took our trash to the kitchen, bringing the box of apple pie with me on the way back.

"I am happy," she countered. "I have a great job, two wonderful kids, and a family that I love."

She pulled her shoulders back defiantly as I held a bite of

apple pie on a fork in front of her.

"Yeah, but do you have someone who gives you orgasms that make your toes curl and makes apple pie that can send you straight to heaven?"

Her eyes studied the fork suspiciously as if I had somehow poisoned it. She parted her lips and took a bite.

I grinned as I watched her struggle to suppress the moan as she chewed and swallowed. Her eyes fluttered closed, and I knew she was in for it.

"Give him one date, Jane. If he can make you feel better than that single bite of apple pie did, then you owe it to yourself to explore whatever this thing is between you guys. And one thing is for sure—at least he's persistent. He's not going to give up easily."

"That's what I'm afraid of," she muttered, wiping the side of her face with a napkin.

"Or is it that you might actually like him too?"

She stayed silent while I set the remainder of the pie on the coffee table and sat on the floor, ready to finish wrapping the rest of the gifts.

Thirty-Six
Nate

I worked Monday and Tuesday, which left me off for Christmas Eve and Christmas day. It was hectic trying to finish up the rest of my shopping, and I spent a lot of time in my office wrapping everything so I would be ready and not scrambling at the last minute.

Capshaw had popped into my office yesterday to ask if Jane or her kids had any food allergies, then left with a smile plastered across his face when I told him I didn't think so. I had no idea what he was up to, but I also didn't have time to stop and ask.

We spent the morning at my parent's house and enjoyed lunch with them before heading to Jane's house for dinner. Abby had insisted on baking desserts for both, but I could tell that she was hurting today after being on her feet for so long yesterday, which made me even more anxious for tonight when I could give her the best part of my gift this year.

Jane was in the kitchen when we got there. Mikey let us in and then followed Sally into the living room, where they were watching *The Grinch*. I helped Abby put the gifts we brought under the tree, then followed her into the kitchen to see what Jane needed our assistance with.

"Everything smells great," I said, smiling when she turned around and wiped her brow with the back of her hand.

"Thank you. Dinner should be ready soon."

Abby leaned up on her tiptoes, checking to see what Jane had cooking on the stove.

"What can I help with?"

"I've got it," Jane insisted with her back to us.

"Jane…"

Abby was as stubborn as her sister, so I stayed on the sidelines and waited until one of them told me what to do.

"Umm," she turned, looking frantically around the kitchen. "We still need to set the table. Other than that, everything is either on the stove or in the oven where it's staying warm until we're ready."

"We're on it," Abby replied, nodding for me to help her get the plates down.

We went about setting the table while Jane finished mashing the potatoes. When we were done, Abby poked her head into the living room and asked the kids to go wash up before dinner. Jane was busy pulling dishes out of the oven and setting them on the trivets on the table when the doorbell rang.

She looked at me with a quizzical look, and I shrugged. I had no idea who was at her house. She tossed the oven mitts to the counter, shut the oven door, and went to answer the door.

I knew she lived in a safe part of town, but that didn't stop me from being protective and peeking into the room.

The voices were mumbled as she held the door partly open, keeping whoever it was from coming inside.

For a moment, I thought it might be her ex, Rick, but then I heard Capshaw's voice, and everything suddenly made sense.

"You didn't need to do this," she said quietly, taking a bottle of wine and the gift bag that he extended to her.

I knew I should pull back and give them privacy, but part of me wanted to see how this played out and whether he had finally taken my advice to just be himself. Sure he was younger than us—and therefore a little rough around the edges still, but he was also a really cool guy who had the world's biggest crush on Jane.

Abby had gone to the other bathroom after sending the kids to wash up and was coming down the hall when she spotted me. Her eyes narrowed in confusion, but I held my finger to my lips, telling her to be quiet as I nodded toward the door.

She turned her head and leaned forward, trying to see who was there. Without missing a beat, she casually walked over to where they were talking and opened the door the rest of the way.

"Capshaw!" she said enthusiastically. "What are you doing here?"

She looked from him to Jane with a smug smile on her lips.

He shoved his hands into the front pockets of his jeans and rocked back on his heels nervously.

"I, um, just came by to drop off a gift for Jane and the kids."

Abby lifted her hand to her heart and tilted her head.

"That is so sweet! Why don't you come inside?" she offered, taking a step back.

"We were just about to eat," Jane said through gritted teeth.

Abby shot her a look but didn't say anything.

"Oh, no, thank you," he replied quickly. "I don't want to interrupt your family dinner. I just wanted to drop that off and was already in the neighborhood."

I covered my mouth and bit back the laughter as Abby nudged Jane in the side with her elbow. Jane sighed and glared at Abby before turning back to Capshaw.

"You're welcome to join us."

His brows rose on his forehead in disbelief.

When no one said anything for a solid minute, I stepped out of the shadows of the hallway and headed toward them.

"You're letting the cold in," I said, grabbing Abby's hand and leading her back inside. "And dinner is ready, so let's go sit down and enjoy the delicious meal Jane prepared for us."

Abby clung to my side, nuzzling her face into my chest as Jane turned and headed to the kitchen. Capshaw nervously came inside and gave me a look that said *what the hell am I doing?*

I clapped him on the back and laughed as he took his coat off and hung it on the rack behind the door.

The kids were already seated at the table when we walked in. Abby and I sat across from them, leaving the seats at each end of the table open for Jane and Capshaw.

Everyone was quiet as we passed dishes around the table, filling our plates.

"Thank you so much for having me," Capshaw said, breaking the silence.

"Who are you?" Sally said, looking up at him with the cutest smile.

"Oh, I'm um," he stammered.

"His name is Jack, but everyone at the fire station calls him by his last name, Capshaw," I answered. "He's one of my friends and a super cool guy."

I rolled my eyes at how dorky I sounded, but Sally seemed impressed nonetheless.

"You're a firefighter?!" Sally asked, her eyes as big as her grin.

"I sure am."

"Wow! I can't believe we have *two* firefighters here for dinner tonight," she said happily.

"Why does that make you so happy?" Jane asked with a grin of her own.

"Because if you catch the turkey on fire again, they can put it out right away."

Jane's face turned red as Capshaw and I tried to look away before she caught us laughing.

"That happened one time, Sally," she corrected with a small laugh. "But I guess I'll never live it down. And to be fair— we didn't have to call the fire department. I was able to put it out myself."

Everyone laughed and ate their food. Once we were done, Capshaw and I kicked the girls out of the kitchen while we cleaned up. I had been to Jane's house plenty of times to know where the majority of stuff went.

"Well, this was unexpected," I said as I washed a plate and handed it to him to rinse and dry off.

"Yeah, definitely not what I had planned."

"What did you plan?"

He shrugged.

"Just to drop off a gift and leave."

I washed the last plate and handed it to him before pulling the plug and letting the dirty water drain out.

"What made you decide to bring her a gift?"

He dried the plate, then set it on top of the others while he thought about it.

"She ordered delivery from Surf 'N Shack on Sunday, and when I saw her name on the order, I volunteered to take it. We talked for a few minutes when I dropped it off, and it felt like she was finally starting to let down her wall with me. It was exciting to think that *maybe* she might give me a chance if she knew I was serious about taking her out on a date. After that, I couldn't get her out of my head and knew I wanted to do something nice for her. I know that you and Abby buy gifts for her and the kids, but I can't imagine that her dick of an ex does anything. And for just a moment, I thought that maybe *I* could be the guy who did something to make her feel special for Christmas. I know it's not much, but I wanted her to feel like someone else cared about her the way she deserves to be cared for."

I smiled and squeezed his shoulder.

"It's great, man; I think it's really sweet of you to want to do that for her."

"It's not just to get in her pants," he admitted with a blush. "I know everyone thinks that that's all I'm after, but it's not.

Jane isn't like other women, and I know that. I respect that."

We finished putting the dishes away and joined the girls in the living room when the doorbell rang again. Jane looked up at me with the same look as earlier, and I shrugged once more. It wasn't like I had some sort of guest list of who would be visiting her house tonight.

Abby was sitting on the floor, her round belly wrapped snuggly in a new dress that I absolutely loved on her. Mikey and Sally sat patiently on the couch while she separated the gifts into piles while Jane went to answer the door.

Capshaw and I sat in the chairs on the other side of the room, staying out of the way. Jane returned with Rick behind her, a smug look etched on his face that I wanted to smack off of him.

"Merry Christmas, everyone," he said with a stiff nod, scanning the room to see who was there. He carried a handful of wrapped boxes and set them down on the floor behind Abby.

"What are you doing here?" Jane asked, hands firmly on her hips.

"I brought the gifts for the kids so they would have them to open tomorrow morning."

"Why didn't you keep them at your house?"

"Oh, I forgot to tell you. Shannah and I are heading out to Ocean City in the morning and won't be home."

Jane's eyes looked like they were about to bulge out of her head.

"What?"

It wasn't a question but more of a statement of disbelief.

"Don't start," he muttered, running a hand through his hair.

"Hey kids, why don't you go get the presents you made earlier? There are extra gift bags in that big blue tote I brought in with me," Abby said, pushing up off the floor. I helped her up while Capshaw stood and glared at Rick.

Once the kids were out of the room with Abby, Jane turned to Rick and narrowed her eyes while clenching her fists at her side.

"You have some nerve," she bit out. "Tomorrow is Christmas, Rick. CHRISTMAS. And you're bailing on your kids to go spend time with your new girlfriend?"

"Like you're one to talk? Bringing some frat kid to the house without telling me about him first?" Rick pointed a finger at Capshaw.

"He's not—" Jane started before Capshaw crossed the room in a few steps and wrapped an arm around her waist.

"A frat kid," he finished for her. "I'm thirty-five, own a house, have a *very healthy* 401K, and know how to treat a woman."

I watched Jane swallow hard as she allowed her body to relax against his.

"Whatever," Rick muttered under his breath. "I brought their gifts; what else do you want from me?"

Jane shook her head but didn't try to pull away from Capshaw as he continued to hold her.

"Nothing. Not a damn thing."

"Fine. I'll take my gifts and go so you can get back to enjoying your family night without me."

"Like you would actually stay if you were invited," Jane snorted. "You want as little to do with this family as possible."

The kids came back into the room with Abby, holding gift bags stuffed with tissue paper.

They handed their father the bags, and I couldn't help but notice the sadness on Sally's face when he didn't bother to seem excited about it as he yanked it from her.

"Don't you want to open it before you go?" Sally asked when he started toward the door.

"Yeah. Sure." He stopped by the edge of the couch and set the bag down before reaching inside and pulling out a bunch of popsicle sticks that were glued together.

He frowned and held it at different angles as he tried to figure out what it was.

"Turn it around," Abby said softly. "It's a picture frame."

He raised a brow at her, then did as she said, still unimpressed by the gift his daughter made.

"Pretty." He tossed it back into the bag and then opened the other.

Mikey sat on the couch, avoiding looking at his dad while he opened his gift. Rick pulled out a baseball and turned it around, finding a signature on the back.

"What's this?" he asked, holding it up for Mikey to see.

"I signed it," he replied with a shrug.

"Oh. Cool." He tossed it back in the bag, not noticing the look on Mikey's face etched with disappointment.

Mikey swallowed hard and turned away. Jane pushed away from Capshaw and went to sit beside him on the couch.

"You need to leave," I said quietly, making sure he heard the tone in my voice.

"I was just headed out," he blew out breezily as if his lack of interest in the gifts his children made him didn't bother him one bit, which it didn't.

I could feel the anger radiating off me once he left, and I hated that he had come over just to ruin Christmas Eve for his kids. I locked the door behind him, making sure he couldn't come back inside even if he wanted to.

Abby held Sally on her lap while Jane tried talking to Mikey before he got up and stormed off to the kitchen. Jane dropped her head into her hands and sat there.

"I'll go talk to him," I offered, not knowing what else to do.

"I'll go with you," Capshaw added. "If that's okay with you, Jane?"

She nodded, looking absolutely defeated.

We found Mikey sitting at the kitchen table, running his finger repeatedly over a groove in the center.

"Hey, buddy," I said, sitting at one end of the table while Capshaw sat at the other. "Want to talk about it?"

"What's there to talk about?" he sneered. "My dad hates me and everything I do."

"That's not true," I started, but Capshaw lifted his hand and stopped me.

"I was around your age when my dad walked out and left my mom and me," Capshaw said softly. "He left Christmas morning and told us that the best gift he had ever been given was the freedom away from a family he didn't want."

Mikey looked up at him with tears in his eyes. This wasn't something I had heard about Capshaw before, but I admired him for opening up to help Jane's son because he could relate to what he was feeling.

"Wow, that's really mean," Mikey replied softly, turning to face Capshaw. "What did you guys do?"

"Well," he sighed, leaning back in his chair. "I cried, and my mom came over and wiped the tears away. She told me that it didn't matter whether he stayed or not. We had each other, and that was all that mattered."

"Was she sad?" he asked. "Did she cry too?"

"I'm sure she did, but she didn't let me see it. Moms are really strong like that. But she did make it the BEST Christmas ever. I still remember it vividly, just like it was yesterday."

Mikey stayed silent for a minute, staring down at his hands.

"Did it make you sad not having your dad around when you were growing up?"

Capshaw paused for a moment, looking up at me as if wanting guidance on how to answer.

"I realized early on that I didn't need anyone who didn't want to be there. My mom was my biggest fan and still is today.

I'm sure it was hard for her to be a single mom and raise me on her own, but I honestly don't feel like I ever missed out on anything. She went to all of my sporting events. She taught me to drive. She was always there for me."

We heard footsteps, and Jane rounded the corner a few moments later.

"Everything okay in here?" she asked cautiously, keeping one hand on the wall as she looked at us.

Mikey pulled his shoulders back and nodded.

"Yeah, everything is good." He smiled, then rushed over and wrapped his arms around her. I noticed the look in Jane's eye as she smiled at Capshaw and held her son. Giving them some privacy, I got up and went to find Abby, desperate to hold her and my sweet baby.

Thirty-Seven
Abby

By the time we finished at Jane's, I was exhausted. Aside from the drama that Rick stirred up, the night was wonderful and we had fun watching the kids open their gifts from us. Jane didn't bother having them open their gift from their dad since they were still in a sour mood and I didn't blame her. They had gotten an ugly look into who he was as a person and didn't owe him a damn thing right now.

Nate and I helped clean up and walked out with Capshaw. I was surprised by how late he stayed, but even more so at how easily Jane had shifted her disposition to him and stopped shooting daggers into the side of his head. She had loosened up some after he got there, but something changed even more inside of her after he sat down and talked with Mikey. I saw something in her eyes that hadn't been there before. Respect.

It was barely after eight when we piled into Nate's truck and got our gifts loaded up. I offered to help, but he wouldn't let me. Instead, I was ushered inside where it was warm and I could be off of my feet. Jane hugged me through the window, squealing with excitement as she wished me a Merry Christmas. Something was up with her, but I couldn't figure out what. She was overly giddy and excited.

Once Nate climbed in, I had the heater vents aimed toward his seat and the cabin nice and toasty. I leaned back against the headrest and closed my eyes for a few minutes, looking forward to going home and crawling into bed.

"So," Nate said, pulling out of Jane's driveway. "We're not heading home tonight."

I opened one eye and turned to look at him.

"We're not?"

"Nope."

"Where are we going?"

"It's a surprise."

He grinned, and instantly I knew that I couldn't be mad at whatever it was he had planned. I eyed him suspiciously, then closed my eyes and rested again.

"It'll be worth it, I promise."

I reached over and squeezed his hand.

I don't know how long we were on the road, but suddenly I was startled awake by a loud snore as my body jolted upright. My eyes flew open, and I reached up to wipe the drool that was sliding down the side of my mouth.

Nate was looking forward, pretending to watch the road while keeping the smile off of his face.

"You okay?" He turned slightly with one brow cocked. He slowed down and flipped on his turn signal.

"Yeah, I must have dozed off. Where are we?" I looked around, seeing nothing but snow for miles and thick woods around us.

"We're almost to our destination."

He kept driving, the sound of the snow-covered gravel crunching beneath us as he approached a cabin at the end of the dirt road. He pulled to a stop and grinned at me.

"We're here."

I looked around, completely in awe, as he jumped out of the truck and came around to help me.

"What is this?" I asked in awe, taking his hand as I climbed down.

"This is my first gift to you," he said, wrapping his arms around me as he led me to the front door. "I rented it for the week and already cleared your work schedule with Sherry before you start to freak out about being gone."

He lifted a fake rock, fetched the key, and unlocked the door. I stepped inside, feeling along the wall until I found the light switch and turned it on. Nate closed the door behind him and joined me as we looked around, checking out our home for the next week.

"This is gorgeous," I beamed, holding my hand to my chest as I walked around the cozy room. It was a small space with the living room and kitchen combined in one, but the floor-to-ceiling windows more than made up for it with the beautiful view of the snow we were sure to see in the morning.

A plush sectional took up most of the living room's space, along with a coffee table, a few side tables, and two full-length bookshelves that enclosed the TV mounted to the wall. Beneath the TV was a gorgeous fireplace that I couldn't wait to cuddle up in front of, and in the corner by one of the windows was a beautiful Christmas tree, already set up with lights and decorations.

We toured the rest of the cabin, finding two bedrooms and one bathroom with a large soaking tub and a walk-in shower. It was big and spacious, which made up for there only being one toilet. At least I could soak in the tub while Nate took a shower if he wanted to. I leaned in closer and realized that the tub was actually big enough for both of us and my enormous stomach to all fit comfortably.

"We should have everything that we need, but if we're missing anything, I can run into town," Nate said as we walked back to the living room. "I checked what I could and tried to plan ahead, but you know something always gets missed."

"You've already been up here?"

"Yeah, I stopped by to bring the groceries, so we didn't have as much to unpack tonight."

"Then why did you leave the key under the rock when we got here?"

He shrugged and smiled. "I wanted to keep the thrill of the surprise and didn't want you to be disappointed that I had already been here."

I reached up and gently caressed his cheek.

"This is a wonderful surprise, and I couldn't be disappointed if I tried. But Nate, you didn't have to do all of this for me."

He spun me around and held me to his chest as his eyes fixated on mine.

"I wanted to, Abby. You're worth this and so much more. And I know that this Christmas has been hard on you, so I wanted to make it as enjoyable as possible."

"Thank you," I whispered, trying to hide the emotion in my voice. No one had ever done something this sweet for me before.

"Now, why don't you go get comfortable, and I'll bring the rest of the stuff in from the truck?" he suggested, letting go of me.

"Rest of the stuff?" I asked.

"Yeah, our luggage and the gifts for tomorrow."

My heart sank as I realized that my gifts for Nate were still at my house, and now I wouldn't have them to give to him until we went back.

"What's wrong?" he asked, his brows furrowing.

"Nothing, I just didn't know you were doing this, and my gifts for you are at home."

"No, they're not," he smiled. "Jane told me where to find them, so I loaded them up while you were taking a shower."

"Oh," I blurted out, surprised by how efficient he was and even more so by how Jane was involved. "Well, she was rather helpful, I guess."

"She also helped me pack your bag, and I'm 90% sure that we got everything you could possibly want or need. *If* we missed anything, there's a store about half an hour away that I can stop into."

I stood there in disbelief, wondering if somehow I was still asleep and had been transported into some alternate realm.

Nate went outside and started unpacking the truck while I looked through the kitchen, taking note of what he had already brought up yesterday. The fridge was filled with food and bottles of water, while the freezer had a couple of pizzas and some ice cream with my name written all over it. Okay, so technically it said—*stay out until I tell you to eat it, Abby*—but same difference.

I felt the chilly wind zip past me as he opened the door and brought our luggage in. I had no idea which suitcase was mine and which was his since they looked identical and I hadn't packed anything. Since we constantly shared a bed whenever we slept over, I figured we would do the same thing here and carried both bags to the master bedroom with the king-sized bed while Nate brought in the rest of the stuff.

"Did you find your pajamas?" he called from the living room while I unzipped the other suitcase, finding my stuff inside. Sitting right on top was a pair of plaid Christmas pajamas with a bow placed on top.

I lifted them and held them to my chest as he came around the corner and leaned against the doorframe, smiling at me.

"Nate," I whispered, knowing that he remembered me talking about how fun it would be to wear matching family pajamas at Christmas with my future kids while reading books and listening to Christmas carols.

He opened his suitcase, lifting the clothes on top to pull out his matching pajamas. He held them up for me to see, grinning when he noticed the single tear that slid down my cheek.

"Go get changed, and I'll meet you in the living room."

I nodded and headed to the bathroom, already needing to pee again. When I was changed, I folded my dirty clothes and put them in a pile under the sink, then looked in the mirror at how cute my stomach looked in the comfy pajamas he had picked for me.

The style had Jane written all over it, and I had no doubt that they were maternity PJs based on how loose they were in all the right spots. They were incredibly soft and lightweight and smelled like my favorite laundry detergent, which meant that Jane had taken the liberty to wash them for me.

When I got to the living room, Nate had already changed into his pajamas, and I couldn't help but check out his muscular body in them. The shirt was tight in spots and hung long enough to cover what it needed to, but not too long to hide the way his ass looked in the snug fabric. I wanted to strip them off of him and do naughty-naughty things that Santa would never approve of.

He was beside the tree, tucking the gifts beneath it when I sat down on the couch. I smiled down at him, wondering how I got so lucky to have such a wonderful man in my life. As my best friend, and maybe as more…

I shook my head to clear the thought, knowing that I would just end up frustrated again that we still hadn't defined whatever this had become between us. It was like we were both acting the part of being in a relationship, but neither of us bothered to say it out loud.

He stood up and looked at the tree with his hands on his hips, taking it all in.

"It looks great," I said.

"Thanks, I'm glad you like it."

I nodded and lifted my hand to hide another yawn.

"Ready for bed?" he asked, planting a kiss on my forehead.

"I don't want to ruin anything else you had planned."

"You're not, I promise. I knew that it would be late tonight, so I didn't plan anything else. But I did grab some milk and cookies if you wanted to leave some out for *Santa*."

"Santa or Nate?" I asked with a coy smile.

"Well, I mean, I wouldn't say no to eating your Christmas cookie." He leaned in and tickled my sides as he ushered me to the bedroom.

✳✳✳

I woke up Christmas morning to the smell of coffee brewing and bacon cooking. I climbed out of bed and made a quick pitstop in the bathroom before joining Nate in the living room.

The curtains were open to a beautiful winter wonderland outside. Everything was covered in pure white snow that had continued to fall throughout the night. The tree was lit, and soft Christmas music floated around us.

Nate was sitting relaxed on the couch with a steaming cup of coffee in one hand with the other spread across the back of the cushion. He looked way too sexy in the damn Christmas pajamas, and suddenly, he was the gift that I wanted to open.

"Breakfast first," he laughed as if reading my mind. He got up, gave me a quick kiss, then led me by the hand to the small table in the kitchen where he had already set out plates for us. I sat down while he served us, watching the way his muscles moved as he leaned across me to set an omelet on the plate beside a stack of bacon. He definitely knew the way to my heart.

We talked and ate, laughing at memories of other Christmases and the things that had gone wrong along the way. It seemed we had yet to have one where something didn't go astray. Last year Jane caught the turkey on fire. The year before that, my mom had drunk too much wine while wrapping gifts and mislabeled half of them. And then there was the Christmas of all Christmases when my dad dressed up as Santa and fell down a flight of stairs, scaring all of the kids in town and starting a nasty rumor that Christmas would be canceled because Santa died.

It felt good to laugh, even if I had to keep squeezing my thighs together to make sure I didn't accidentally pee a little. Things felt normal again, and I loved that I had this time with Nate. Even though it was completely different than any other Christmas I've ever had, it still felt special and magical, which was what I needed.

After we finished eating, I cleaned up our dishes while Nate worked on my next gift. It turned out that he had set everything up with Jane and my parents to do a Zoom call so we could all celebrate Christmas together, even if none of us were in the same spot. I cried when I saw my parent's faces show up on Nate's laptop and then cried harder when Jane and the kids showed up a few seconds later.

My parents gave us updates on their trip as they held hands, and my dad constantly brushed my mom's hair out of her face for her, something he used to do a lot when I was growing up. She peppered his face with kisses, and for a moment, I had to look away to keep my breakfast down. I loved that they had rekindled the spark that had started to die out, but there was only so much mushy-gushiness between my parents that I could stomach.

We stayed on the call for over an hour before Jane needed to go so the kids could finish opening their gifts. I was eager to give Nate his as well, so we said goodbye and promised to do another call on New Year's Eve. I felt instant happiness with my heart overflowing thanks to Nate.

"You are unbelievable," I said as he disconnected from the video and shut down his laptop.

His brows rose in surprise, and I could tell that he wasn't sure if that was meant as a compliment or an insult.

I laughed and patted his arm.

"In the best way possible," I added. "I cannot believe how much you've done for me to make this day special. Thank you so much. I don't think I will ever be able to tell you how much this means to me."

"Just like I'll never be able to tell you how much *you* mean to me," he whispered, leaning in to kiss me. "You've already given me the best gift I never knew I wanted." He rubbed his hand over my stomach and smiled.

"Well, now you've added an insane amount of pressure that my real gifts will never measure up to," I joked, getting up from the couch and sitting beside the tree as I scanned the gifts for the first one I wanted him to open. "But we'll start with this and see where we get."

I handed him a box wrapped in shiny gold wrapping paper with a red bow wrapped around it.

"Thank you," he said, grinning as he gently pulled the ribbon to undo the bow. He lifted the lid, and his eyes popped open as he reached in to lift the stack of vinyl records out.

"Abby," he breathed, flipping through them. "How did you find these?"

"It turns out Colin has a friend who recently inherited a large collection from his dad. These were going to be sold in an estate sale, so I grabbed them before anyone else could."

"These are incredible; thank you so much." He set them back in the box and then reached over to hug me.

It warmed my heart to see how happy he was. I knew these were the ones he needed to complete his collection and had been hard to find. Even better, they were still sealed and appeared to be in immaculate condition.

Nate reached around the tree and handed me a large box wrapped in an assortment of mismatched paper. He shrugged and said, "It was the last gift I had to wrap, and I ran out of paper that would fit."

I laughed and opened it, finding a beautiful wooden box inside. I pulled it out and set it on my lap, knowing that this was something special by the way Nate was watching me.

Inside was a beautiful photo album with ivory-colored satin stretched around it. I lifted it out of the box, noticing another album beneath it. I glanced at Nate, feeling his eyes on me as I gently turned to the first page and felt my heart skip a beat.

There were ultrasound photos of the baby with the date of each one listed in the journal area beside it. After that, there were pictures of Nate and me when we first met, and I laughed when I found the picture of me standing next to him wearing a t-shirt that said *Saturday*, which no doubt matched the underwear I was likely wearing as well. Our childhood spanned across the pages until I got to the end and found recent photos of us.

Some were of Nate and me together that we had posed for, but there were a handful of just me that he had taken without me knowing. Some of me while I was sleeping, some of me laughing or making silly faces, and a lot of me holding my stomach as I looked lovingly at *our* baby.

"Since we don't know if we're having a boy or a girl, I had them make it gender-neutral. It's the baby's first photo album that they'll always have to know how much mommy and daddy always loved each other."

I reached up and wiped the tears away with the backs of my hands.

"It's beautiful," I cried, holding it to my chest.

"There's another one, but it's for you, not the baby."

I set the first album down beside me and picked up the other one. This one was wrapped in black leather and had a picture of me with my grandparents in the pocket on the front. I lifted it closer, noticing that it was taken the day they had officially signed over Rockin' Rooster to me, and we were celebrating with cups of hot chocolate and my grandpa's famous apple turnovers.

I opened the album and cried harder when I found all of my favorite pictures neatly organized on the pages with dates and quick notes about what each photo was. I covered my mouth to hide the sob that escaped me.

"The original photos are in the envelope," he said, nodding to the bottom of the box.

I looked up at him, unable to see him through the tears that were covering my eyes. He had taken all of the photos that I treasured and had them restored for me so I wouldn't ever lose them. I clutched both albums to my chest and felt myself tremble with emotion.

"This is the best gift ever, thank you," I said when I could finally catch my breath.

"You're very welcome."

We hugged and then put my albums somewhere safe while we finished opening the rest of our gifts.

Nate loved the sweaters I had picked for him, along with a new brand of dark roast coffee that I knew he would enjoy. I was ecstatic over his reaction to the vinyl records I had found but found myself even happier when I saw how much he loved the coffee tumbler that said *caution, I'm hot*. It was truly who Nate was and showed his sense of humor.

Besides the amazing albums Nate had made for me, he also spoiled me with a foot spa so I could soak my feet without having to balance on the side of the bathtub, some relaxing lavender lotion that made my skin feel amazing, a wine glass that said *mama's happy juice*, and several boxes of snack foods including mixed nuts and delectable chocolates he picked up at the holiday festival.

Once all of our presents were opened, I helped him clean up the trash and put everything away. I was already feeling tired, which was frustrating but not surprising.

"Alright, your next gift for the day is to lay down on the couch and watch a movie with me," Nate said, grabbing a blanket from the basket on the floor.

"There's no way we're both going to fit on that," I laughed, eyeing it suspiciously. It was a big couch, but my belly would make it hard for both of us to fit the way we used to.

He raised a brow and moved around me, pushing the coffee table out of the way before he lifted the cushions and pulled out the sleeper bed.

"Ta-da!"

"Wow, I had no idea that was in there. I'm impressed."

"I thought you might be," he joked, patting me on the ass as he passed by me.

A few minutes later, he had everything set up with pillows and blankets galore. Then he lit a fire, turned on a movie, and held me while I drifted asleep and he watched Die Hard.

Thirty- Eight
Nate

Christmas had been as relaxing and wonderful as I had wanted it to be, and Abby seemed over the moon about having the cabin to ourselves for the entire week. There was no stress over work or having to rush off anywhere. We could do what we wanted, when we wanted, without having anyone to answer to, and that was an incredible feeling.

After her nap that afternoon, she helped me get Christmas dinner ready. It was fun cooking with Abby and laughing as she accidentally sprayed me with milk as she turned on the mixer for the mashed potatoes. It was different than the other holidays we'd spent together, with everyone on edge and stressed about making it the perfect day. For us, it was still a perfect day because we were having fun and not worried about anything other than eating delicious food and spending time together. I loved every moment of it and couldn't wait to show her the rest of the stuff that I had planned for us for the week.

"How are you feeling?" I asked, rubbing her feet as she laid on the couch against a huge pile of pillows.

"Tired," she yawned. "Sore."

"I told you to let me handle the kitchen stuff. You shouldn't overdo it."

"I'm fine. I can't just sit around on my ass all day. It's going to get even bigger than it already is."

I leaned over and pretended to check it out.

"Looks fine to me."

I winked and settled against the cushion, rubbing my thumb against her arch. She reached over and playfully swatted at me.

"Like you would complain anyway," she laughed.

"Not in a million years. The bigger it gets, the more I have to hold on to as I take you from behind."

The grin tugged at my cheeks as I noticed the blush creeping up her face. I loved that even after all we had done together, I still had that impact on her.

"Well, it doesn't sound so bad when you say it like that."

"That's because it's not. You're beautiful, and I love every single inch of your perfect body."

She smiled and wiggled her toes.

"How about a bath?" I offered, knowing she needed to soak so she wasn't overly sore tomorrow. I wanted her to enjoy her time and didn't want pain to damper anything.

"Are you going to join me?" she asked, raising her eyebrows suggestively.

I tilted my head and pretended to think about it for a moment.

"A hot, naked girl in a bath filled with lavender-scented bubbles…. That's a tough decision."

I jumped up and let her feet hit the cushion where I had been sitting before extending a hand to help her up.

"Come on, let's go," I urged excitedly.

She laughed and waddled to the bathroom, not fighting me as I pulled her shirt up and over her head on the way. I was already almost entirely naked by the time we got to the tub and turned the water on while she finished undressing. I had read a few books and researched online to see how hot of a bath she could take. I knew that pregnant women weren't supposed to take hot baths, but the general consensus was that a warm bath was fine as long as her blood pressure didn't get raised.

I rushed off to grab the bath salts I had purchased and read the directions on the back for the hundredth time before sprinkling some into the water.

"You okay over here?" she asked with a laugh, looking over my shoulder as I read the label again.

"Yeah, just making sure I'm putting the right amount."

"I think it's fine," she confirmed, leaning over slightly to look into the tub.

"I asked the woman at the store, and she said they were safe for you to use but recommended not using a lot at once until we knew that you didn't have a reaction. Everything is organic, and I checked the list to make sure that it was okay for pregnant women. I just didn't want the scent to be too overwhelming for you. Is it okay?"

"It's perfect."

She smiled and held my hand as I guided her into the bath. The sweet scent of lavender floated around us as she slipped under the bubbles. Once she was situated, I climbed in behind her and pulled her to my chest as I cradled her stomach in my hands. Her head rested against my chest, sending up notes of coconut from her shampoo.

"This feels so good," she whispered, her eyes closed as her head fell to the side, allowing me the perfect view of her breasts.

I tried to ignore how my cock twitched beneath her, but she was right—this felt good. Too good. I shifted beneath her, trying to keep my overly excited dick from poking her in the ass. He had good intentions, but the goal was for her to relax and have a nice soak.

"He misses me," she teased, practically reading my mind.

She reached down and grabbed my cock, stroking it firmly in her hand.

"He definitely does."

"What are we going to do about that?"

"What would you like to do?" I asked, my voice gruff and strained.

She turned her head and watched me, never breaking eye contact as she continued to jack me off in the water. Then, without warning, she turned her body and threw her leg over my waist, straddling me.

I reached up and grabbed onto her waist, helping to guide her over my cock so she didn't slip and get hurt. She licked her lips as she held onto the side of the tub and allowed me to pull her down, lining my throbbing dick up at her entrance.

"Ahh," she moaned as it slid inside her, gliding effortlessly as she rocked down. "I think I like this position."

"Me too," I grunted, feeling like I was seconds away from coming undone. It wasn't like we had gone a long time without having sex, but something about having her in this position felt incredible and had me curling my toes to keep from coming.

"I feel like I'm weightless," she laughed, riding me while I continued holding onto her and guiding her movements. "I could ride you like this all day, every day."

"Remind me to buy us a soaking tub for the house when we get home," I muttered, closing my eyes.

She giggled and pushed down even further, taking me fully inside of her. I could tell by the way her thighs started clenching around me that she was close.

"Touch yourself," I panted, opening my eyes to watch her. I wanted her to come, but I wasn't willing to let go of her to bring her to orgasm myself. The last thing I wanted was for Abby to somehow get hurt during sex in the tub.

She leaned back slightly, allowing herself room to rub her clit. I shifted beneath her, making sure I was still as deep as possible, thrusting inside of her while she worked herself. The water sloshed around us, spilling over the side of the tub as we both climaxed.

"That was amazing," she murmured, falling against my chest and resting while we both caught our breath.

"Everything with you is amazing."

I trailed my fingers up and down her back, gently caressing

her body which was still hyper-sensitive. There was more that I wanted to say to her, confessions that had been on my tongue for weeks but I couldn't manage to get out. I told myself that it would be a Christmas gift to myself to come clean to her and tell her how I felt, but when she squeezed me tighter and nuzzled her cheek against my chest, I knew that I couldn't. As much as I loved Abby, I wasn't willing to break my own heart if she didn't love me the same way.

Thirty-Nine
Abby

"So, what else did you guys do?" Jane asked, lifting her coffee cup to her lips. "Other than screw each other senseless for a week while the rest of us had adult responsibilities to handle."

I rolled my eyes and popped a bite of cinnamon roll into my mouth.

"We built a snowman, went into town, and did some shopping. Then, he took me to this charming restaurant for dinner on New Year's Eve. It was so much fun, and the owners were super friendly. They surprised us with a custom dinner menu since we were the only customers they had that night. We ended up staying until midnight and counted down with them."

"That sounds like fun. I'm glad you had a great time together."

"Thanks, me too. I didn't want it to end."

"I wouldn't want it to either," she laughed. "It sounds like it was a dream come true."

I swallowed my bite and looked away, trying to avoid how her words had hit my heart like a torpedo. The problem was that it felt just like a dream—perfect and everything that I could ever wish for, but it wasn't reality, and I needed to remember that.

It was a wonderful week, but it ended at that. When we came back to town, everything went back to normal. Well, almost everything. Work was waiting for us, and while we were gone, Colin's dad had lost his battle with cancer, which meant that there was a lot of planning that I needed to do to help his family with his dad's services.

We had talked a few times about having Rockin' Rooster cater the wake, but we still needed to sit down and figure out the menu. It wasn't just about having food for everyone; it was about honoring George and the wonderful man he was. I had suggested preparing all of his favorite foods, and while Colin protested at first, he came around when I confirmed that I would have help getting everything done.

"So, how are things with you and Capshaw?" I asked, deciding to turn the attention away from me.

"Fine, I guess. Nothing happened after Christmas Eve."

"You didn't exchange numbers? Hang out? Ring in the new year together?"

"No," she laughed and took another sip of coffee. "Not everyone has fairytale dream romances lined up in front of them," she teased.

"You could if you tried. Capshaw would move heaven and earth for you, Jane. If you'd just let him."

"It's not that easy." Her shoulders fell with a sigh while she held her cup with both hands and lowered her eyes.

"Why not?"

"Because I'm a single mother with an asshole for an ex, and he's still a kid himself."

"He's hardly a kid," I countered.

"He's six years younger than me with no baggage."

"You act like you're some kind of burden, and you're not. You have kids, so what. They're amazing, and he seemed to really like spending time with them while he was there."

"Maybe he was just pretending."

"Why would he do that?"

"I don't know," she shrugged helplessly. "To get me to let my guard down so he could get in my pants."

"I think he has better things to do," I laughed, noticing the way the corners of her mouth turned up as well.

"Either way, it doesn't matter. I'm too busy with work and the kids to try to start a new relationship, and Rick finds a way to squander any joy that I find anyway."

"Well, then we deal with Rick. He's seeing someone new anyway. Maybe he should focus on his own happiness instead of trying to destroy yours."

"Ha! That'll be the day," she snorted.

I shook my head, knowing that she was right.

"So, when is your next appointment?" Jane asked, switching the table back to me again.

"I have another ultrasound on Wednesday."

"Seven months already. Soon *she'll* be here, and I can't wait to squeeze and cuddle her!"

"We don't know if it's a girl," I laughed.

"I do. It's totally a girl."

"And how exactly do you know that?"

"I just have a feeling." She shrugged and batted her eyes.

"We'll just have to wait and see." I smiled and rubbed my stomach, convincing myself for the hundredth time that I wanted to be surprised in the delivery room and that I didn't want to find out before then.

"I guess so," she sighed and stood up. "Well, I'm headed to work, but I do need you to think about the baby shower and let me know what theme you guys decided on so I can get started on it."

"Do we really need a theme?" I walked with her to the counter, waving at the customers who were leaving.

"You don't *need* one, but I think it would be fun. Plus, you only get to have one baby shower; why not make it the best?"

"Because it's a lot of time and energy and work."

"Yeah, but you're not the one who has to worry about all of that. I want to do this. Please let me?" She held my hands between hers while she begged with her eyes.

"Fine, I'll talk to Nate later and see which one he likes best."

"And then you'll talk to him about whose house you guys are going to live in so you can stop this nonsense of pretending like you're not together when you really are, and you're both madly in love with each other but are too chicken shit to admit it?"

"Funny," I muttered, shaking my head at her. "Don't you have a job to get to?"

She laughed and pulled me in for a hug before planting a kiss on my cheek.

"Talk to you later."

I nodded and watched her leave. I knew she only wanted the best for me, but I hated that it wasn't something I could ever have.

<u>Forty</u>
Nate

My head was spinning after I walked out of my Chief's office with an offer that had just about knocked the wind out of me. He had spoken with the Chief in Ocean City, and it seemed my name was thrown in as a good candidate for the Battalion Chief position that had recently opened. While there were no guarantees that I would get it, I had been asked to go down there next week and meet with him.

I rushed around the station, getting my stuff ready so I could head over to Rockin' Rooster as soon as my shift was over. I couldn't wait to tell Abby the good news. It was something that I had wanted for as long as I could remember, and I knew that she would be relieved that I wouldn't be running into fires anymore—something she's always not-so-secretly hated about me being a firefighter.

By six-thirty, I was still riding my high of possibly taking the next step in my career when Capshaw came into my office and sat down with a shit-eating grin on his face.

"So, should we start calling you Battalion Chief Wilson now?" he asked as he leaned back into the chair.

I tried to keep the smile off of my face but failed miserably.

"The job isn't mine yet."

"You know you're going to get it. You're the best guy for the job."

"There are a lot of highly-qualified candidates," I countered, pointing my fingers into a steeple and tapping them together.

"Yeah, but you're the only one with years of experience and education to back it up. You've taught everyone here and the majority of those in the small towns around us. Give yourself more credit than that, Captain."

I inhaled slowly and then let it out, trying not to get my hopes up too high just yet.

He was right, though; I had trained most of the Beaumont Creek firefighters and the neighboring towns. It wasn't that we had the best platoon around, but we were highly sought after for helping out when needed. I had spent the past eighteen years learning everything I could and training myself to be the best of the best.

"How do you think Abby will take the news?" he asked.

"I'm sure she'll be happy about it," I answered without thinking about it.

He raised his brow in quiet disagreement, then shrugged.

"What?" I laughed. "Why wouldn't she be excited about it? I'll finally be working from the sidelines and not running into burning buildings—it's a win/win for both of us."

"Yeah, except that the position isn't in Beaumont Creek. It's in Ocean City. Three and a half hours away."

I sat there for a moment, hearing what he was saying but failing to process what it really meant.

"I know, but it's not like I'll be moving there. I'll drive down for my shifts, and it really won't be any different than it is now."

"Except if she needs you, or the baby needs you, it'll take hours before you can get to them. Do you think she'll be on board with having you so far away with a newborn to take care of?"

My shoulders slumped as I realized what he was saying. I had promised Abby that I would be there for her and that I would jump in and help whenever she needed me. While I had more flexibility here in town if there was an emergency, I knew that wasn't the case if I took the job in Ocean City. Abby needed me to keep my promise, and that meant that I couldn't consider taking the position.

"Fuck," I muttered and pushed away from my desk. "I hadn't thought about any of that."

"Who knows," Capshaw said with a smile. "Maybe she'll be cool with you taking it? She has her parents and Jane here, so it wouldn't be like she didn't have any support while you were gone."

I nodded but didn't feel any better about it.

"Just talk to her," he urged. "You'll never know unless you guys sit down and discuss it."

I chuckled, knowing there was more left unsaid by the tone in his voice.

"Yeah," I sighed. "I'll talk to her later and see what she thinks."

By the time our shift ended, my mood had soured, and the excitement of Battalion Chief was nowhere to be found. I wasn't mad about it, just more frustrated that I hadn't thought about how it would impact Abby and the baby before I got my hopes up. *How had I been so selfish that I hadn't considered putting them first?*

I had been back and forth with trying to convince myself that we might be able to make it work and that Abby might even be on board with spending a few days in Ocean City with me when I went for my shifts. It would still be 48 hours on and 72 off, so it might be doable with some creative finagling of her schedule—if she was willing. I could sell my house in Beaumont Creek and get a place in Ocean City for us, so she and the baby would be comfortable. Then, again, if she was willing—I could ask her about moving in with her and the baby since I wouldn't have a place in Beaumont Creek if I sold mine. It was a bit presumptuous of me to ask her for such a large favor and to uproot her life as she knew it, but what if it ended up working for us?

The light out front of Rockin' Rooster was turned off, but the inside lights were still on when I pulled up. I knew that Abby was closing and had texted her to let her know that I was stopping by, though she never responded.

I parked the truck by her car in the back of the lot and headed to the front door. Just as I was about to pull it to see if it was unlocked, I looked up and found Abby and Colin in a warm embrace behind the register. I tried to convince myself that it was just a friendly hug between friends, but when she pulled away from it and his lips lowered to hers, I knew that I was wrong. I clenched my fists, watching as Abby kissed him back, then turned and walked away.

Away from Abby. Away from the dreams of a future with her. Away from everything that had come to matter so much to me over the past few months.

Forty-One
Abby

"What in the world was that?!" I shrieked, backing away from Colin and wiping his kiss from my lips.

"Oh my God, Abby, I'm so sorry." He covered his face and backed further away from me. "What the hell is wrong with me?" he muttered, pulling his hair through his hands in frustration.

I took a few deep breaths and tried to steady myself. We had spent the past hour reminiscing about our childhood and growing up together while sharing stories of his dad. That all circled back around to our *almost* engagement and how things would have been different if he had stayed. I couldn't say that I blamed him for what had just happened, but it definitely caught me by surprise.

"Nothing is wrong with you," I blew out and leaned against the counter behind me. "There's a lot of emotion floating around right now." I twirled my finger in the air between us.

"Yeah, but I knew better. I know you're with Nate, and I respect that, Abby. I really do."

I lowered my head and stared at my swollen feet, knowing that I needed to get off of them soon.

"We're not together," I admitted sheepishly.

"You're not?"

"No." I took in a deep breath and slowly let it out. "We're just friends who are having a baby together."

He turned and stood next to me, crossing his ankle over the other while resting against the counter.

"But…. You love him. And he loves you."

I could hear the confusion in his voice and hated that it stung straight through to my heart.

"It's not that kind of love."

"For you?"

I paused and thought about it even though I already knew the answer.

"It's difficult."

"Abby," he sighed, letting his head fall back. "You have to tell him."

"I can't."

"Why not?"

"Because," I laughed nervously, turning to face him as I pushed away from the counter. "We agreed that this would be just a one-time thing between us. He would help me have a baby, and that was it. We never talked about being in a relationship or falling in love with each other."

The words were falling out of my mouth as quickly as the tears rolled down my cheeks. Gently, he reached up and brushed them away with his thumb.

"You might not have been trying to fall in love, but you did anyway."

I covered my face and cried. I knew it was true—heck, probably everyone else already knew it. But hearing the words come from Colin's mouth was my undoing.

"How did you know?" I asked, my words mumbling against his chest as he pulled me into a hug.

He rubbed my back soothingly before answering me.

"Do you really want to know?"

I nodded.

"Well, it's because I recognize the look in your eye."

I pulled back slightly, allowing his arms to stay wrapped around me, and looked up at him.

"I have a look in my eye?"

He grinned a toothy smile and bobbed his head up and down.

"You do. It's the same look you used to give me before I left."

My heart sank, and the tears started all over again.

"Don't cry, Abby," he said softly. "I didn't say that to upset you. I just meant that I've seen the sparkle that lights up your whole face when you're in love. Even if that sparkle isn't there for me anymore, I love seeing that you still have it for someone else. Especially Nate. I knew that he would look out for you and take care of you when I left. You both deserve this love that you're trying so hard to fight."

He let go of me while I turned and grabbed a box of tissue from the shelf below the register. I quickly wiped my eyes and then shifted away from him to blow my nose.

"Nate doesn't love me like that," I said sadly, looking up to find sympathetic eyes searching for something in mine.

"Are you sure about that?"

I shrugged and nodded.

"It's okay; it wasn't part of the plan to begin with. I was stupid for thinking that he could possibly fall in love with me. I was always like his pesky little sister that he had to take care of."

He arched a brow and folded his arms over his chest.

"Okay, maybe not like a sister anymore, but still. Not love. Nate doesn't do love or commitment. Never has, and I don't think he ever will."

"You'll never know unless you talk to him about it. You owe it to yourself to at least have that conversation with him, Abby. I've seen the way he looks at you, and if I didn't know better, I'd think he's been in love with you longer than you could imagine."

I tried not to get excited about the idea that Nate could be in love with me. While we should have talked about things between us a while ago, it was always easier to just go on as if nothing had happened. We were just friends who had sex so I could have a baby. Even when the sex didn't stop, we didn't question what this thing between us was. Maybe things would have been different if we had, or maybe Colin was wrong, and it would have pushed Nate away and freaked him out if he thought I tried to trap him and get him to commit to me when I knew that wasn't something he wanted for himself.

One thing was for sure—I wouldn't know unless I grew a pair and talked to him.

Colin stuck around for a bit to help me lock up, then walked me to my car. We had a plan for what foods I would make for George's services which was progress compared to the huge pile of things he still had on his plate to take care of.

I had seen a missed text from Nate saying that he was on his way over to Rockin' Rooster, but when he hadn't shown up by the time we were getting ready to leave, I got worried. On my way home, I called him, but it went straight to voicemail. I left a message apologizing that I hadn't seen his text and that I was heading home if he wanted to come over.

By ten o'clock, I still hadn't heard from Nate. I was about to go looking for him when my phone rang.

"Hey," I answered, sounding too sullen to pass it off as just being pregnant and cranky.

"What's wrong?" Jane asked, her mom tone coming out in full force.

"Nothing," I sighed heavily as I picked at the pieces of lint on the blanket covering my lap. "I haven't heard from Nate all night, and I'm starting to worry something happened. He sent a message saying that he was heading to my work but then never showed up. I've called and texted him since then but nothing."

"Oh, maybe he's just out celebrating with the guys and didn't hear his phone."

"Celebrating what?" I frowned, wondering what she knew that I didn't.

She paused as if realizing that this wasn't news she should be sharing with me.

"Spit it out, Jane."

"I don't think I should be the one to."

"Well, it seems everyone already knows about it if you do."

"It's not my fault, I heard from Capshaw."

"Are you guys seeing each other now?"

"No, we just ran into each other at the grocery store. I was picking up stuff for dinner, and so was he."

"And did this result in you guys having dinner together?" I teased.

"Haha, funny. No, I'm at home eating dinner by myself, and he's wherever doing whatever because it's none of my business."

"You're so stubborn."

"Guess it runs in the family," she chided happily.

"Okay, so tell me—what are they celebrating?"

She let out a very loud, very heavy breath.

"Nate is being considered for Battalion Chief."

"What?!" I jolted forward in surprise.

"In Ocean City."

Her words knocked the joy right out of me as soon as I registered what they meant. Nate was leaving, and he hadn't bothered to tell me.

Forty-Two
Nate

Things with Abby had been odd when I first left for Ocean City, so it didn't surprise me any that they hadn't gone back to normal in the month that I had been here. Was there even a normal for us anymore?

After I caught her and Colin together, I decided that I would do what was best for everyone and walk away. Abby deserved to be happy and have the family life she's always dreamed of, and Colin seemed to be the perfect guy to make that happen for her. While I hated that I wasn't going to be as involved in my baby's life as I had initially thought, I reminded myself that I loved them enough to step away and allow them to have the family that Abby gave them.

It was already approaching Valentine's Day, which meant that Abby was a month away from her due date and likely soaking up all of the loving, romantic gestures that Colin was dolling out for her. I didn't bother to ask anyone for updates on how she was doing and walked away anytime someone mentioned Beaumont Creek.

While it wasn't my original plan, I decided at the last minute to rent my house back home so I didn't have to go back and forth to Ocean City. It was wonderful to have been selected for the Battalion Chief position, and I had to constantly remind myself that *this* was the dream that

I'd always wanted for myself. Not the family life with a beautiful wife, adorable kids, and a home that smelled of freshly baked goods. Some people could have it all, but I wasn't one of those people.

I was the guy who lived his life doing what he loved without any commitment. The guy who got the thrill from running into a burning building and who felt an insane sense of pride and satisfaction when I was able to save someone from a fire. I wasn't built for the cuddly, soft side of life. I was made for the lonely, bachelor style who could check out once his shift was over and not worry about anyone needing anything from him until he was on shift again.

The problem with drinking at eleven in the morning on a Saturday was that there wasn't enough alcohol to truly make me believe the shit I was trying to convince myself of while I sat by myself in a lonely studio apartment with nothing on the walls and bare minimum furniture. My parents had stored all of my valuable items for me so I wouldn't have to worry about them being lost or damaged by the new guy renting my house. He seemed nice enough, but we never fully trusted new transplants in a small town.

Even the alcohol couldn't block the memories of the fight that Abby and I had right before I left. It was a last-minute decision to move to Ocean City, and it was as well-received as everything else that came out of my mouth.

Abby paced back and forth across her kitchen with her hands on her hips, brow furrowed.

"So that's it, you're just leaving?" she asked, throwing her hands in the air.

"I got offered a position that I've dreamed of since I was

little. You know how much that means to me." My jaw tensed as I spit the lies at her. I hadn't been offered the job yet, but I was determined to go and not come back until it was mine. I needed a break from everything in Beaumont Creek, and Abby needed a break from me. Only then would she be able to see clearly what had been standing in front of her all along.

"I thought maybe this meant something to you, but I guess I was wrong." She pointed to her stomach, then shook her head and turned away to keep me from seeing the tears well in her eyes.

My heart ached at how hurt she was. I never wanted her to feel that way. But I knew what I needed to do, and it sucked that it had to be this way. She deserved better than I could ever give her. Some day she would see that.

"I don't know what you want me to say, Abby. We agreed that it would be just one time. We would make a baby— which was what you wanted. We never talked about this being anything more."

The words burned my throat and made my stomach churn. They were lies, all lies.

"Fine. Go."

She turned and stormed out of the room, leaving me to let myself out. With my heart in pieces, I pulled myself together and walked out of her house and out of her life forever.

I was flipping through the channels on the TV, trying to forget that night, when my phone rang. Tilting my head slightly, I saw my mom's name flash across the screen but made no effort to answer it.

A few minutes passed by before it rang again. And again.

Finally, I grabbed it and pressed it to my ear.

"What."

"Nathaniel James Wilson, I know you do not think that is how you speak to your mother," she scolded sharply.

"Sorry, I didn't see the caller ID," I lied.

"You know damn well that you saw my name. That's why you didn't answer the first four times I called."

Touché.

"The reason for my call," she continued when I didn't say anything, "is to see if you're planning on coming to town next weekend for the baby shower. I can make up the guest room here, or if you'd rather stay with Abby—"

"Don't," I snapped. "I'm not coming for the baby shower. I've told you that at least a hundred times already."

She sighed with disappointment. I hated a lot of things in life these days, but the one that I hated the most was knowing how much I had let her down.

"Would you please just stop with this pity party you're having and come home?"

"No can do."

I could almost hear the fire coming out of her head. There was a faint noise on the other end of the line, then suddenly, I heard my dad's voice.

"Why do you always have to upset your mom before dinner?" he joked. "You know she's going to burn my steak now that she's off in a tizzy."

"Hey, she called me."

"Because she's worried about you. We all are."

I shifted on the couch, lifting my butt to pull out whatever was crinkling between the cushion beneath me. I frowned and looked at the candy wrapper, trying to remember when I had eaten it and, even worse—how long it had been stuck in the couch. I tossed it to the coffee table and continued scrolling through the channels.

"You still there?" he asked, probably hoping that I had hung up and he could tell my mom that at least he'd tried.

"Yup." I let the p pop at the end.

"What's going on with you, son? This isn't like you at all."

I closed my eyes and pinched the bridge of my nose between my fingers.

"Nothing, dad. I'm fine. If people would just trust me when I say that, then they wouldn't have to worry about me."

"No one has seen you since you took that position in Ocean City. We miss you."

"I'm not that far. People can drive up here if they want to."

I knew what they were always after—getting me to go back to Beaumont Creek. Everyone had it in their heads that if I went back and saw Abby, I would stay, and we would be this beautiful, happy family. But the problem is that none of them had seen the way she kissed Colin. I knew Abby better than anyone, and that meant that I had to do what was right for her.

"I don't think the entire town is going to be able to come up there at one time," he joked.

"Yeah, well, I doubt the whole town wants to see me, to begin with. The only time everyone comes together like that is for weddings, funerals, and the holiday festival. Since none of those are happening right now…."

"Alright, fine," he conceded with a sigh. "But we do miss you here."

"I miss you too, dad."

"If you change your mind, the baby shower is next Saturday at one. Colin is hel—"

"Thanks, dad. I won't be able to make it."

I hung up before he could say anything more. Abby had Colin; what more could she possibly need.

Forty-Three
Abby

"Jane!" I squealed, hugging her tightly as I looked around her living room at the beautiful decorations she had made for my baby shower. "This is beautiful! You did such an amazing job!"

"Thank you," she smiled, holding my hands in front of her. "But mom helped too."

"Mom?" I raised my brows and started scanning the room for her. I knew she and my dad were due back from their trip any day, but I hadn't seen them yet.

They were originally going to come back for George's service, but Jane and I convinced them to "attend" via Zoom instead since my mom had caught a cold, and we didn't want her to travel while under the weather. We also didn't want to risk her getting worse or bringing whatever it was back with her.

Suddenly, my mom came down the hallway and yelled *surprise* with my dad in tow behind her.

"Mom! Dad!" I rushed over and wrapped my arms around them. "I can't believe you guys are here! When did you get back?"

"A few days ago," my mom answered, gently brushing a strand of hair off of my face. "We've been helping Jane with the party and wanted it to be a surprise."

"I'm definitely surprised," I laughed, rubbing a hand over my belly as the baby kicked me.

"You okay?" my dad asked, nodding to my ginormous stomach.

I nodded.

"Baby has been kicking up a storm since I got here."

"She's probably hungry," Jane called from the kitchen.

"We know it's a girl?" My mom raised her brows.

"No, Jane is just convinced it's a girl. We won't know until the baby gets here."

"Only a month to go," my mother said as she rubbed her hand over my bump.

"I can't wait," I replied, letting her and my father rest their hands firmly on my stomach while they waited for the baby to kick again.

Jane came back in a few minutes later with a turkey and swiss cheese sandwich wrapped in a napkin.

"Here, eat this before everyone gets here. You might not have much time to enjoy your food since you're our guest of honor, and I want to make sure you don't get hangry."

I took the sandwich but furrowed my brow.

"I don't get hangry."

Six eyebrows rose and judged me accordingly.

"Okay, fine, whatever," I laughed, then took a bite.

I sat down on the couch and propped my feet up on the

coffee table, thankful that my dress was long enough that I didn't have to worry about sitting too ladylike. The baby took up so much room and was so low that it made it uncomfortable to try to close my legs.

There were red and white balloons hung throughout the room and a few that were tied together to make ladybugs. I had totally forgotten to tell Jane what theme Nate and I had decided on because he had left town, and I hadn't heard from him since. It had been an intense month with lots of crying and throwing things at the wall when I realized that whatever was going on with Nate and me was long over. I knew what becoming Battalion Chief meant to him, but I was stupid to think I could ever possibly be more than that.

"The theme is love bug," Jane said proudly when she noticed me taking in all of the decorations. "Since the party was on Valentine's Day, we thought it would be cute."

I smiled and took another bite of my sandwich before answering, "it's adorable."

"Don't worry, not everything is red and white," she assured me. "Just the throw-away decorations. Everything else was picked with gender-neutral in mind for the gifts."

"Is Nate coming?" my mother asked, coming back into the living room with a bouquet of flowers that went with one of the centerpieces on the gift table.

"I don't know."

"You still haven't heard from him?" Jane questioned softly as she sat down beside me.

I crumpled my napkin and dropped it on my lap, staring down at my pregnant stomach. *His baby. Our baby.*

"His mom said he's busy with work and was on shift today, so he couldn't make it."

"Well, that's too bad. We'll miss having him here," my mom answered, then went back to the kitchen to help my dad.

"I hate this for you," Jane muttered, leaning against the cushion beside me. "Why are guys so stupid?"

"He's not stupid; he just went after what he wanted. No one should blame him for doing that."

"But he didn't even ask what *you* wanted, Abby. You guys are having a baby together, and he just up and left."

"I know," I nodded sadly.

I still remembered in vivid detail the night we talked about it. Nate was angry, and I couldn't figure out why. Then he told me that he had been offered the Battalion Chief position in Ocean City and had decided to take it. I asked what that meant for us, and he just shrugged.

I had read in my pregnancy books that soon-to-be fathers sometimes freak out right before the baby is born, and I assumed this was what happened with Nate. Since we had agreed to do this as friends and nothing more, I didn't want to complicate things by bringing feelings into it. If Nate wanted to walk away and open the next door to his future, he should be able to. I didn't want to be the one to hold him back from doing that.

"It's just not fair," she continued.

"It doesn't matter. He's in Ocean City doing what he's always dreamed of, and that's what I want for him. A life where he's happy and calls the shots. He wouldn't have been happy staying here and playing father to a child that he never thought about having before I came into the picture. It wasn't fair of me to ever expect that from him."

She turned to face me, and we rested our heads on the cushion as we looked at each other.

"I'm really proud of you for doing this on your own," she said.

"I'm not on my own," I laughed. "I have you. Mom. Dad. I have a team."

"Colin?" she pressed, squeezing my hand.

"As a friend, yeah. But nothing more than that."

It was true, that night after he kissed me, we talked about it and then laughed when neither of us felt anything. It was a bit of a relief to know that it wasn't just me and that he wasn't secretly holding feelings for me that I couldn't return. We agreed to be just friends, and ever since Nate left, he was one of the best friends I could ask for.

Colin had taken a permanent position at Rockin' Rooster and was training with Sherry to handle more responsibilities when I went on maternity leave. His father's service had gone smoothly, and we had been asked about the possibility of catering other events in the near future. When we realized how much of a math whiz Colin was and how easily he could plan things, we put him in charge of setting up some catering items for when I got back.

"Well, we can never have too many friends, and speaking of which, it sounds like they're here." She jumped up off of the couch and went to answer the door while I struggled to fight gravity to get up.

The baby shower was fun, but by the end, I was tired, sore, and desperately wanted to go home and climb into bed. I thanked everyone as they left and then waited while my parents helped Jane pack up the gifts and load them into my dad's truck so he could unpack them as soon as I got home.

Throughout the day, I couldn't shake the disappointment that Nate wasn't there and that he was missing out on all of the love and happiness that people felt toward our sweet little baby. The longer I thought about it, the more I realized the emptiness that I felt with not having him here anymore. It wasn't just his friendship that I had lost; it was a part of me that he took with him.

Forty-Four
Nate

Abby had sent me a few pictures from the baby shower, and I replied with a thumbs up and smiley face emoji, unsure what else to say. My mood had stayed sour all day, hating that I hadn't gone when I knew how much it meant to her.

But then I also knew that Colin would be there and would jump in to help her build the furniture for the nursery. *Their nursery*. Not only was he there to pick up wherever she might need it, but her parents were back from their trip according to the social media posts her mom was tagged in, showing her smiling next to Abby as she hugged her and held her hand over hers on her stomach.

It was late for Abby to be up still, but that didn't stop her from sending me another text message.

Abby: I wish you could have been there today.

I chewed the inside of my cheek and debated how to respond. Everything that came to mind was snarky, and she didn't deserve that from me. That was one of the reasons I had avoided going back to Beaumont Creek—no one deserved to have to deal with my piss-poor attitude right now. Though I wasn't sure it would be much better any time soon. Things were only going to get worse once Abby had the baby and Colin settled into his new role as a *father*.

Me: Me too.

There, simple and not dickish. It was the best she was going to get from me right now.

Abby: How are you doing?

I lifted my beer to my lips and snorted. That was a loaded question.

Depressed. Angry. Bitter. Horny. Frustrated.

Me: Fine. You?

I knew that if we kept texting that she was going to know something was wrong with me. That was just how Abby was—the knower of all things and reader of people. Okay, so maybe that was the beer attempting to talk, but still, she knew me better than anyone.

As if predicting that she wouldn't get anywhere with me via texts, my phone rang in my hand.

I stared at her picture as it flashed across my screen. I wanted to talk to her more than I was willing to admit, but I knew that it would be better for everyone if we kept our distance right now. I still needed time to process how I felt about her and Colin, and frankly, I wasn't in any position to do that with the amount of beer in me.

I ignored the call and sent her a text instead.

Me: Sorry, headed to bed. Talk later?

I watched as the dots bounced across the screen, waiting for her to respond.

Abby: Okay.

It didn't take a genius to know that she was mad at me, but at the end of the day, I would rather have her be pissed at me than hurt by me.

The next two weeks passed by in a blur. I went to work, put in the hours, and then spent any free time I had working out or running. It seemed that no matter how hard I tried, I couldn't burn off enough frustration. I knew that it was because of how I left things with Abby, but there was no way to fix it without talking to her, and talking to her meant there was a chance that I would slip up and let things go back to the way they used to be between us, and I couldn't let that happen.

I was finishing my shift when I got called into the Chief's office.

"You asked to see me," I said, knocking on the door before stepping inside.

"Yes, come in and close the door."

I swallowed hard and did as instructed.

"Have a seat." He nodded to the empty chair and waited for me to sit.

I took a deep breath and sat down.

"I'm not going to beat around the bush, so I'll just get straight to the point."

I swallowed hard and nodded.

"You've been distracted lately, and it hasn't gone unnoticed. Unfortunately, in our line of work, we can't afford distractions. So I need to know whether you can do this job or if I need to look for someone else."

Fuck.

I rested my ankle on my knee and tapped my fingers nervously on my shoe.

"I'm sorry, Chief Goodwin. I assure you it will not happen again."

I looked him in the eye, wondering if he had read through the bullshit I had just tried to throw at him.

It wasn't that I was trying to lie to him; I just couldn't guarantee that I wouldn't be distracted given that Abby was two weeks away from popping my baby out and starting a new life without me.

"I've seen that look before," he warned, looking down his nose at me.

My shoulders rose and fell with the sigh that escaped me.

"What's going on?"

"I don't know," I muttered. "I'm sorry for being distracted. I don't try to bring my personal business to work with me. I'm better than that. It won't happen again," I tried to reassure him.

He pushed away from the desk and stood up, looking out the window behind him.

"Do you know why I brought you on board as a candidate for Battalion Chief?" he asked, keeping his focus on a bird hopping around the ground looking for food.

I stayed silent, too afraid that I would confirm that he made a mistake by bringing me on.

"Because you reminded me a lot of myself when I was your age."

He turned and faced me, the features on his face softening a touch.

"Determined. Career driven. Focused. I knew what I wanted, and I went for it. Come hell or high water, I was going to have whatever I set my sights on."

I tried to smile, but it fell short.

"Sometimes what we think we want isn't what we need, and when those two lines get blurred, it can create a *distraction*."

I pulled in a deep breath and slowly let it out, praying that it would give me the strength I needed to keep the shakiness out of my voice when I spoke.

"This is all that I've ever wanted, Chief Goodwin. I apologize for letting you down so early on, but I will make sure I do better from here on. You have my word."

He nodded but didn't look like he believed a word I said.

"You're off shift for 72 hours. I strongly recommend you take that time to do a little *soul-searching*. Think about what you want out of life and see if that still matches what you thought you wanted. You'd be surprised how much can change without you realizing it."

I got up and locked eyes with him.

"Yes, sir."

I left feeling more uncertain about everything than I had ever felt before.

Forty-Five
Abby

"Are you still balancing that bowl on your stomach?" Colin asked, joining me on the couch.

"I've gotten really good, look." I pointed to how perfectly it was sitting on my belly.

"I'm surprised you haven't woken the baby up with all of that sugar."

"I think it's in a sugar coma," I laughed. "I'm sure I'll pay for having ice cream this late when I'm kept up all night with kicks to my bladder."

I rubbed a hand over my incredibly tight stomach and wondered how I hadn't popped yet. My finger trailed lazily over my belly button that was pulled flat across my stomach and technically no longer existed.

"What time is your appointment tomorrow?" he asked, resting his feet on the coffee table.

Hanging out with Colin had become the new norm for the past few weeks after I fell into a depression that no one could easily pull me out of. While he wasn't Nate and wasn't trying to be, it was still nice to feel like I had someone who was there for me the way Nate used to be.

"Eight, but I have to check in a few minutes early."

"Do you want me to take you?" he offered.

"I'm good going on my own but thank you."

He nodded but didn't press it any further. I knew that he wanted to be there for me in all aspects of my life, but it was hard for me to let him be there for me when it came to stuff with the baby. Part of me wanted to keep that spot saved for Nate, not that he wanted it. But the other part knew deep down that I couldn't go down that road with Colin. It wasn't fair to either of us to pretend to have this family together when we knew that we weren't right for each other anymore. The last thing that I wanted was to allow myself to depend on him and then hold him back from starting a family with someone else. He deserved happiness, and so did I.

"I think I'm going to head to bed," I said, grabbing the bowl and attempting to get up.

It was like wearing a sumo wrestling suit—I was so big and round that I couldn't easily stand up on my own without assistance these days.

I grunted and set the bowl on the table beside me, then pushed off the armrest and made my first attempt to stand up. Colin looked away and rubbed his lips together to keep from laughing. By the third attempt, I'd managed to lift myself off of the couch but couldn't help but wonder if the fart I'd accidentally let out didn't help push me with the force of it.

Colin got up quickly but didn't say anything about the chemical warfare I'd just released on him.

"Yeah, I'd better get going," he rushed out in a single breath.

Guess that was one way to clear the room and let him know it was time to leave.

I walked him to the door and then locked it behind him. The empty house reminded me of the loneliness that I'd felt since Nate left. No matter how hard I tried, I couldn't fill the void he'd created.

The next morning, I walked into the doctor's office irritable and grumpy from another restless night of tossing and turning. I had also run out of the delicious decaf coffee that Nate had been buying for me, which made me even more of a morning demon.

I checked in and took a seat in my usual spot. My stomach was tighter than normal this morning, so I had to shift a few times before I was comfortable. Finally, after moving eighty times and debating throwing the chair through the window, the nurse came to take me back to the exam room.

Doctor Nicoli came in a few minutes later, which was why I loved taking the first appointment of the day. While I didn't love getting up early to get here, I did appreciate not having to wait long since I was rarely comfortable these days.

"How are you feeling?" he asked as he sat down on the stool and typed in his password to unlock the computer screen.

"I'm ready to pop."

He laughed and glanced at me before typing something.

"It could be any day now," he commented as he continued to type. "Have you started feeling any signs of labor?"

We had been discussing what to look for at each visit since I was now coming to see him once a week. However, since Nate wasn't there anymore, it was up to me to know what to expect and look for.

"Nothing that I've noticed," I said, then winced and grabbed my stomach.

He turned and studied me, watching where my hands were holding on as I held my breath until the pain passed.

"Contraction?" he asked as he walked over to where I was sitting on the exam table.

"I'm not sure," I gritted out. "But it hurts."

He put his hand where mine was and kept it there until the pain subsided.

"I'd like to do a physical exam if you're okay with it."

I nodded and let out a slow, steady breath as I sat up straight, thankful that the pain had subsided. He opened the door and spoke to the nurse that had checked me in, asking her to return to the room when she was done checking the next patient in so she could be present for the exam.

I knew that it was probably just Braxton Hicks since he had already told me that they could feel a lot like real contractions. I still had almost two weeks left until my due date, give or take. From what I'd read online, a lot of first-time moms went past their due date, so I wasn't expecting to be one of the rare ones that went into labor early.

A few minutes later, the nurse returned and closed the door behind her. I was already changed and ready for the exam when Doctor Nicoli joined us.

"Okay, Abby, go ahead and scoot down as far as you can," he instructed while the nurse hovered next to me in case I needed help. Once I was situated, I closed my eyes and tried to focus on something else while he did the exam.

I was trying to conjure up an image that would soothe me, but all I could see was Nate's stupid face. Knowing my luck, the baby would come out looking exactly like him, and I would have to see it all the time.

"It looks like that was a real contraction," he said as he pulled away from me and tossed his gloves into the trash. "You're already 70% effaced and dilated three centimeters."

I sat upright on the table and stared at him in disbelief.

"What does that mean?" I asked stupidly. I knew what it meant but needed to hear him say it.

"It means that you're in labor and having a baby. Congratulations!"

My head started spinning as the nurse talked to me about moving me to a labor and delivery room and something else about calling someone for me. I tuned her out as all of the blood rushed out of my head, causing everything to go dark.

Forty-Six
Nate

"I'm sorry, what?" I said into the phone in disbelief.

"Abby is in labor; we've moved her to the delivery unit. She's resting, and we're monitoring her contractions, but I wanted to let you know since she hasn't been able to get to a phone since she found out."

"I'm on my way." I didn't wait for a response and hadn't bothered to get the girl's name when she called. All I knew was that Abby was in labor, and they'd called me. Why they called me, I had no idea, but part of me hoped that it was because she had asked them to.

It was the start of my seventy-two hours off shift, and I was about to do the deep, hard thinking that Chief Goodwin had asked me to do. Little did he know that it was going to take place on the freeway as I hauled ass to get to the woman that I loved.

I didn't give anyone a heads up that I was coming before jumping in to my truck and speeding to get to her. It was a three-hour drive from Ocean City back to Beaumont Creek, but if I were lucky, I would do it in two.

I wanted to call Abby and check on her but reminded myself that I wouldn't be able to focus on the road if I was on the phone with her. Instead, I put on a soothing jazz station that I loved and tried to force myself to relax. The last thing that

Abby needed while trying to give birth was a stressed-out me showing up and ruining the experience for her.

After an hour of driving, my cell phone rang with a call from my mom. I pressed the button on the steering wheel to answer it through Bluetooth so I could talk hands-free. See—I was already doing well with minimizing distractions.

"Hello," I answered casually as if I wasn't doing ninety on the freeway to get to Abby.

"So, I have some exciting news," she squealed.

"Oh yeah?" I replied coyly, feeling the smile tug at my lips. "So do I."

"You go first," she insisted.

"No way, ladies first."

"Well, I got a call from Abby's mom that she's in the hospital in labor!"

"I know," I said happily. "I'm on my way."

"Nathaniel James Wilson!" she shrieked so loud that I tried to pull away, but the sound encompassed the cab of the truck. "Why didn't you call and tell me?"

"Because I was just focused on getting to Abby."

She was quiet for a minute, so I checked to make sure the call hadn't dropped.

"I knew you'd come back," she whispered.

"Well, at least one of us did."

I don't know what had changed in me, but the moment I got

the call from Doctor Nicoli's office asking me to come be with Abby, I knew that was exactly where I needed to be. Suddenly it didn't matter that she was with Colin or that they were going to start a new life together. Abby was as much a part of my life as she was his, and I would fight until she agreed to let me be part of this new chapter of her life, even if that meant that I needed to walk away as Battalion Chief.

In the blink of an eye, everything had shifted, and I could see what I really wanted. Maybe it was the brief chat with Chief Goodwin, or maybe it was literally getting a wake-up call—I had a rough night the night before, and it was my day off, sue me for wanting to sleep in a little. Either way, I felt like I finally knew what I needed to do. I pressed my foot to the gas and prayed that I wasn't too late.

Forty-Seven
Abby

"Do you want an ice chip?" Jane offered from beside the bed.

I narrowed my eyes and glared at her as another contraction released its vice grip on me.

"Not unless it's in the form of a fish and chips from Surf 'N Shack," I growled.

"Sorry, my friend, but no food. Doctor's orders."

I muttered a few choice curse words and turned my attention to the soap opera on the TV. One woman was yelling at another woman while the man stood by, smiling like he was proud of the drama he had created. Suddenly one reached out and slapped him, forcing the smug grin off of his face before the other got her turn.

I laughed and wondered how satisfying that must have felt.

"Don't even think about it," Jane said, pointing to the TV. "Hangry or not…."

"It's not fair," I whined. "I didn't even get breakfast this morning. Pregnant women need to eat. The baby needs food, Jane."

She raised a brow and planted her hand on her hip.

"*She's* hungry, Aunt Jane, not me." I pushed my bottom lip out and let it tremble slightly for dramatic effect.

She rolled her eyes and sighed heavily.

"Let me go talk to Doctor Nicoli."

I smiled and clapped my hands as if I'd won some huge achievement.

Ten minutes later, she still hadn't come back. My guess was that they got caught up *talking* again, which honestly looked a lot like flirting to me, but what did I know. I was starting to get annoyed again when the door opened.

"If you don't have fish and chips, then leave because I'm not afraid to eat your head and feast on your brain," I called out before the privacy curtain was pulled back.

My heart skipped a beat, and my stomach dropped when I saw that it was Nate, not Jane.

"I don't have fish and chips, but I also advise against consuming human flesh," he said cheekily as he shoved his hands into his pockets.

I narrowed my eyes, trying to see if he was really there or just a figment of my imagination. When he came closer and squeezed my foot under the blanket, I knew he was really there.

"What are you doing here?" I bit out, suddenly fueled by the anger that had been building up toward him over the past month.

"I got a call from the hospital letting me know that you were in labor, so I came."

"You shouldn't have. And they shouldn't have called you."

His face fell along with his shoulders. I knew that he was on the list of people to call when I went into labor if he wasn't already with me. First Nate, then Jane, then my mother. Unfortunately, I hadn't remembered to update the list and had forgotten about it until now.

"Abby," he breathed, slowly lifting his eyes to find mine.

"No. Don't you *Abby* me. Do not come in here acting like nothing happened."

The monitor beside my bed started beeping as my blood pressure rose with my anger. I clenched my fists and closed my eyes as a contraction gripped my stomach.

"Are you okay?" he asked, coming to my side and reaching for my hand.

"Contraction," I managed to blurt out as I yanked away from him.

I waited for it to be over before I opened my eyes and found him standing further away from me with his hands back in his pockets.

"Is it over?" he questioned quietly.

I nodded and stared at the TV.

"Why are you really here?"

He sat down in the chair beside me and rested his elbows on his knees. His hair was longer than it was the last time I had seen him, and there was a new scruff that dotted his normally clean jawline. The bags under his eyes meant that he either just got off shift or he hadn't been sleeping well. At least I wasn't the only one.

"I messed up, Abby. I can't begin to tell you how sorry I am, but I hope you'll eventually allow me to make it up to you. When I saw you kissing Colin, I lost it. I know I didn't have any right to be upset about it, but that didn't stop it from killing me."

I pulled my head back in surprise and then turned to look at him.

"You saw us kiss?"

He nodded and lowered his head between his hands before taking a deep breath and sitting up straight to talk to me.

"The night that I texted you that I was heading over to your work. You didn't text me back, so I went ahead and showed up. Right as I was going to open the door, I saw you guys behind the counter kissing. I knew he could give you the life you've always wanted, so I left. I thought I was doing the right thing, Abby. Moving out of the way so you wouldn't have to decide who you wanted in your life."

I leaned my head against the pillow and closed my eyes. Suddenly, everything made sense. Why he hadn't shown up that night. Why he was so angry at me after that. He had been there and seen a kiss that looked like something more than it was.

I covered my head with my hands and groaned.

"We are so stupid." I shook my head and looked at him.

"Well, I am, but you're not."

"No, I'm stupid. I should have connected the dots all along but didn't. God, this makes so much sense now," I laughed, feeling some of the anger slowly dissipate.

"What are you talking about?"

I shifted as much as I could in the bed, given that I was attached to what felt like hundreds of cords that went to different monitors.

"I waited for you to show up that night and got worried when you didn't. When I mentioned it to Jane, she told me that you were probably out celebrating the new position you were being considered for."

"Why would I be out celebrating when I didn't even know if I was going to get it?" he asked with brows pulled together.

"Exactly!" I said a little too enthusiastically. It was like solving a murder mystery that had haunted me for weeks, and now I had the missing pieces. "You wouldn't do that but I didn't think about any of that. I was just upset that everyone knew about the offer, and I didn't. I was so hurt that I had to find out from Jane and assumed that you didn't want to tell me yourself because you knew I would be upset if you left."

"I was headed to your work to tell you. But then I saw…."

"Everything was such bad timing," I confirmed. "You saw a kiss that lasted all of three seconds and was instantly regretted by both of us."

"What?" His jaw dropped as he leaned forward and the light suddenly appeared in his eyes again. "I thought you guys had decided to get back together after that kiss."

"No, we didn't get back together. That was never on either of our radars, Nate. While we might have questioned what would have been if he never left, it wasn't like we just picked up where we left off once he got back. We've become really good friends, but we both agree that our past should stay exactly where it is—in the past. We're different people, and neither of us feels any chemistry with the other anymore."

"I can't believe it." He leaned back and covered his mouth as his grin spread across his cheeks. "I thought for sure you guys have been together this whole time, planning the rest of your lives as a happy family."

"Nope. In fact, I've been helping him set up his online dating profile while he helps me build furniture for the nursery."

"Wow. I really messed this up, didn't I?"

I sighed and reached my hand out to him.

"We both did. If we would have sat down and talked about things, none of this would have happened to begin with."

He squeezed my hand and refused to let go.

"Well, since we're talking now, there's something that I need to tell you."

Butterflies danced in my stomach as I waited for another contraction to come in and mess it up.

"I love you, Abby," he said with a sigh. "I'm madly in love with you, and being away from you made me realize how much I need you in my life. Without you, I'm nothing, Abby. I'm this pitiful mess of a man who has nothing in his life that makes me happy."

A tear slid down my cheek as my eyes clouded with emotion.

"I love you too, Nate. More than I ever knew was possible."

He got up and sat next to me on the edge of the bed, holding both of his hands in mine.

"I know that I've screwed up and that you don't owe me anything, but please tell me we can go back to the way we were before. I need you in my life, and I want to be part of my baby's life. I want to be a daddy and a *boyfriend* if you'll have me?"

I started to nod eagerly until a contraction shot through me and killed the romantic, fairytale moment we were trying to have. *Fucking contraction.*

Forty-Eight
Nate

"Push," Doctor Nicoli instructed as he reached down to help guide the baby out. "Another push, Abby. You're doing great."

I held Abby's hand as she pinched her eyes shut and pushed.

"If you want to see, now is the time to look," Doctor Nicoli said, locking eyes with me for a brief second before returning his focus to Abby. "She's starting to crown."

I looked at Abby, unsure of what she wanted.

"You can look."

My palms were sweating, and I was nervous even though Abby was the one doing all of the hard work. She let go of my hand and gripped the sheet instead while I went and stood next to the doctor. The nurses moved to the side and got things ready as I took my place and watched the baby's head as it pushed through Abby. It was amazing, and I couldn't take my eyes off of the wonder before me.

Abby groaned and cursed as she continued to push. A few seconds later, the baby was out, and Doctor Nicoli laid it on Abby's chest.

My heart leaped in my chest at the sight of my baby, and my throat felt like it was burning as I tried to force the tears away.

"Congratulations, it's a girl," Doctor Nicoli said, patting me on the back.

"A girl?" I confirmed, standing next to Abby and staring down at the sweet baby in her arms.

Abby was crying, which led to me crying, and soon, it felt like it was just the three of us in the room. A few nurses moved around but didn't rush Abby to give them the baby right away.

"She's beautiful," Abby cried, rubbing her finger gently against the baby's cheek.

"Just like her mama." I bent over and went to kiss her forehead at the same time she looked up at me.

Our lips brushed against each other, and suddenly, everything in the world felt right again. I didn't want to ever stop kissing her and hated how stupid I had been the past few weeks.

"Do you guys have a name picked out?" One of the nurses asked, smiling at us as she stood at the end of the bed.

I looked at Abby, knowing that we hadn't talked about it.

"Ummm…" Abby hesitated.

"What name did you like?" I asked. I already knew that I would love whatever she picked.

"I was thinking Penny Mae," she said nervously. "Penny after my grandmother and—"

"Mae after mine," I finished for her. "It's perfect, Abby. I love it."

"It's a beautiful name," the nurse agreed and wrote it down on a laminated card that she taped to the whiteboard on the wall. "Last name?"

We looked at each other again. There was so much that we never talked about before the baby got here that we should have. Like feelings and being in love and what last name the baby would have.

"Wilson," Abby confirmed, then smiled at me.

My heart felt like it was swelling with pride and love and a million other things I never knew were inside of me.

The nurses took the baby for a few minutes to do the stuff they needed, which gave Abby and me a few minutes to talk. I sat on the edge of the bed beside her and wrapped my arm around her shoulders as she leaned into me.

"How are you feeling?"

"Tired. Sore. Hungry," she laughed.

"I'm sure you'll be able to eat soon. I'll ask the nurses when they're done."

"I can't believe she's here. She's so beautiful and perfect. And her little cry is so sweet." She turned and looked up at me with tears in her eyes. "How can I love someone so much when I just met them? It's crazy, but I would do *anything* for her, no questions asked."

"I know the feeling." I wrapped her in my arms and hugged her tightly.

The nurse brought Penny back a few minutes later and placed her in my arms. I held her against my chest and stared at her beautiful face. I now knew what Abby was talking about. This love was different. It was all-consuming. Pure. It was the kind of love you didn't have to question—it just existed. And from that moment on, I knew that I would go through heaven and hell to give both of them whatever they wanted in life.

Epilogue
Abby
Two Months Later

"Do you know where the bottle brush is?" I called to Nate from the kitchen. The sink was piled with dirty dishes, and I couldn't find my own head at this point.

"I think it's in the bottom of the sink," he answered, walking in with Penny asleep on his chest.

"Why don't you go sit down, and I'll take care of the dishes?"

"You've got Penny, it's okay."

"You do know that I can put her down, right?"

I laughed and let the dishes slip out of my hands as he slid an arm around my waist and pulled me in for a kiss.

"You better be careful; you know that I finally got the all-clear from Doctor Nicoli," I warned. Technically I had it two weeks ago, but then I got sick and hadn't been in the mood for anything.

"Don't tempt me; you know I have no restraint when it comes to this sweet ass," he growled and grabbed a handful.

I giggled and wrapped my arms around his neck, gently hugging him without squeezing our lucky Penny.

"Did you still want to go to Jane's for dinner tonight?" I asked, stepping away from him when Penny started to squirm. She wasn't a fussy baby by any means but definitely didn't like to be hot. I was worried that we were in for a hell of a summer with this little girl since it was just barely starting to heat up.

"I'm good with going if you are. I'm sure they'll love to see Penny."

I laughed and bobbed my head.

"They can't get enough of her."

The past few months had gone by in a flash, with many changes along the way. It turned out that life with a newborn was more exhausting than Nate and I had imagined, and it made sense to move in together since we were officially a couple. He was able to move back to the fire station in Beaumont Creek, even though that meant that he had to give up the Battalion Chief position. He assured me that it didn't matter to him anymore; he had everything he wanted in life right here in Beaumont Creek.

Nate moved in with me after I was released from the hospital, which made the most sense since I already had the nursery set up, and he was renting his house to the new nurse at Jane's office. The guy seemed nice, but we didn't see much of him around town. The only time I heard anything about him was when Jane would talk about how young and attractive he was, which had all of the single moms in a frenzy when they would bring their kids in for appointments.

Colin had been promoted to Uncle Colin and was taking full reigns with the catering side of Rockin' Rooster now that I had officially returned to work. He and Cindy went on a few dates, but they seemed to fizzle out as quickly as their attraction started.

I swear, since my parents returned from their trip, they were completely different people. Getting away was the best thing that ever happened to their marriage. My mom no longer tried to interfere in my life and had stopped criticizing everyone she met. She smiled, and for once, I actually believed that she was happy. My dad, on the other hand, had the most change out of all of us. He was more relaxed and carefree than I had ever seen him. Maybe it was the constant fishing adventures that my mother joined him on, or maybe it was that they were planning future trips together. Either way, I loved seeing the happiness that radiated from them.

Penny stirred and shot her arms out as she tried to get comfortable. Nate gently bounced her and patted her back until she settled again.

I smiled at him and felt my heart skip a beat when he winked at me. If someone had told me that I could find love by having a one-night stand with my best friend, I would have told them they were crazy. The only thing that I was wrong about was that it wasn't just one time. It was forever.

• •

Thank you so much for reading Just One Time! I hope you enjoyed Abby and Nate's story. If you want more on Jane, her second chance at love is coming next! https://books2read.com/u/4Aj6Z0

• •

Looking for another series to binge read that will keep you on the edge of your seat? Check out my small-town romantic suspense series, The Haven Brook series. It's steamy and will have you guessing what will happen next! You can find the first book here: https://books2read.com/u/m2RJNR

Other Books By Samantha Baca

<u>The Haven Brook Series:</u>
'Til Death Do Us Part (Haven Brook Book 1)

https://books2read.com/u/m2RJNR

The Cradle Will Fall (Haven Brook Book 2)

https://books2read.com/u/b6O0QE

The Ties That Bind (Haven Brook Book 3)

https://books2read.com/u/mqgoz8

A Very Haven Christmas (Haven Brook Book 4- Novella)

https://books2read.com/u/mvqGjj

Three Strikes, You're Gone (Haven Brook Book 5)

https://books2read.com/u/mvqL2z

<u>The Dark Shadows Series</u>
Five Steps Ahead (Dark Shadows Book 1)

https://books2read.com/u/38Q0gO

Ten Seconds Too Late (Dark Shadows Book 2)

https://books2read.com/u/3JRgVB

Against The Clock (Dark Shadows Book 3)

https://books2read.com/u/m2YwoR

Out Of Time (Dark Shadows Book 4)

https://books2read.com/u/4DKMoP

The Stone Creek Series (Novellas)

Chocolate Covered Mistletoe (Stone Creek Book 1)

https://books2read.com/u/3LRk9N

Candy Coated Promises (Stone Creek Book 2)

https://books2read.com/u/mldP5Y

Pumpkin Spiced Possibilities (Stone Creek Book 3)

https://books2read.com/u/bojdwV

Beaumont Creek Series

Just One Time (Beaumont Creek Book 1)

https://books2read.com/u/3G52zK

Second Chances (Beaumont Creek Book 2)

https://books2read.com/u/4Aj6Z0

Third Time's The Charm (Beaumont Creek Book 3)

https://books2read.com/u/b5lEyG

Four-ever Single (Beaumont Creek Book 4)

Preorder link coming soon

Fifth Wheel (Beaumont Creek Book 5)

Preorder link coming soon

Standalone Books

One Last Wish

https://books2read.com/u/mqg7D9

Finding Love In Apartment 2C (Novella)

https://books2read.com/u/bze9aZ

Cocky Counsel: A Hero Club Novel

https://books2read.com/u/31Kzkn

Something To Talk About

https://books2read.com/u/4X62ag

All Is Fair In Food And War

https://books2read.com/u/bp8qjX

Holiday Books

Snow Place To Go

https://books2read.com/u/4A560N

A Christmas Wish

https://books2read.com/u/4EKXpE

Blame It On The Mistletoe

https://books2read.com/u/bw1rqe

Holiday Hijinks

https://books2read.com/u/4DP6Ze

JUST ONE TIME

Acknowledgments

It is always such an exhilarating feeling to finish another book and bring these wonderful characters to life. Without wonderful readers like you, I wouldn't have a reason to keep writing so thank you so much for taking a chance on me and my books.

To my incredible alpha readers- Azucena, Stephanie, and Amanda—you ladies were amazing with your support and feedback that you provided along the way. I can't imagine doing this without your input and encouragement when I want to throw my laptop against the wall. Thank you for always being there to cheer me on and pushing me to finish the story.

To my street team, thank you so much for your continuous support and for sharing so many of my posts to spread the word about my newest book baby. You all go above and beyond for me and I'll forever be grateful.

To my parents and sister, thanks for always supporting my dreams and pushing me to keep going. I love the random check ins to see how I'm doing and what I'm working on. You've been there every step of the way and I can't imagine walking on this journey without you.

My sweet girls, thank you for letting mama have some time to write the stories that are stuck in my head that you're too young to hear. Trust me—you're doing both of us a favor! Someday when you're old enough to read my books, I'll make sure you have your own signed collection. I'll probably also book a trip across the country with your father so I don't have to be around when your jaws drop at the things your mother has written about!

Dick is short for Richard but I can guarantee you that my husband is anything but. He's the most caring, generous, supportive person that I know and he never ceases to amaze me each time he drops everything he's doing to help me when I need it. Thank you for letting me bounce ideas off of you while asking you randomly inappropriate sexual questions, you never bat an eye and have yet to call me that crazy lady. Or at least not to my face! I appreciate everything you do for me and how much effort you put into helping me with my books.

To all of the readers, bloggers, and everyone that signed up for an ARC of this book—thank you so much for choosing my book and for helping me with early reviews and promotion. None of us authors could do this without you. I'm forever thankful for you!

About the Author

Samantha lives in the southwest with her husband and two small children after abandoning her childhood dream of living in a cabin in Colorado when she found that she couldn't afford to live there and was deathly allergic to the woods. When she's not writing, she's usually spouting off sarcastic remarks while drinking wine out of a coffee mug to look like a functional adult while chasing down her toddlers. She enjoys spending time with her family, watching reruns of Friends, and the 24/7 flow of coffee that can be found in her veins. Be sure to follow her on social media for updates on what she's working on.

You can find her here:

Facebook: https://www.facebook.com/AuthorSamanthaBaca

Instagram: https://instagram.com/author_samantha_baca

Goodreads: http://www.goodreads.com/authorsamanthabaca

Facebook Reader Group:

https://www.facebook.com/groups/2945710968775398/

Webpage: https://authorsamanthabaca.wordpress.com

Newsletter: http://eepurl.com/g0NcSj